I0543738

The Lands Beyond the Moon

The Lands Beyond the Moon

R.W. Schmidt

Wandering Harbor
© **2014**

Copyright © 2014 by Randal Schmidt

All rights reserved. This book or any portion thereof may not be reproduced or used in any manner whatsoever without the express written permission of the publisher or author, except for the use of brief quotations in a book review, and as specified below. Enquiries concerning reproduction permissions should be sent to the Rights Department, Wandering Harbor Publishing Company at the address below.

Illustrations by Randal Schmidt. Some illustrations adapted from public domain artwork. While the original artwork remains in the public domain, the adaptations are copyright of the author and publisher and may not be reused without permission.

Exceptional permission is given to professional primary and secondary school teachers in the United States of America to reproduce brief sections (less than 30 pgs) of this book for use in an educational classroom setting only.

First Printing: August 2014

ISBN-10: 0692261737

ISBN-13: 978-0692261736

Library of Congress Control Number: 2014913866
Wandering Harbor Publishing Company, Frost, Texas

Wandering Harbor Publishing Company
301 E. Pace St.
Frost, Texas 76641

www.randalwilliamschmidt.com

This novel is a work of fiction. All characters in this novel are fictitious. Any resemblance to actual events or locales or persons, living or dead, is entirely coincidental.

If you purchased this book without a cover you should be aware that this book is stolen property. It was reported as "unsold and destroyed" to the publisher and neither the author nor the publisher has received any payment for this "stripped book."

FIRST PAPERBACK EDITION

To Brett and James,
with all my Love

And

In memory of my best friend,
Corporal Mark Raymond Goyet, USMC
Killed in Action
Helmand Province, Afghanistan
June 28, 2011

Preface

Although I want to clarify certain ideas about this story, you would not hurt my feelings if you skipped this preface altogether. I have never liked prefaces in books, so I will keep this one brief.

In simple words, this is a Christian book because its author is Christian.

The values represented herein, and certain assumptions that I make (that life is worth living and worth preserving, that friends are more valuable than gold, that Virtues are both objective and to be desired, and this whole notion of Redemption and reclaiming a usurped throne, of dying to Live) are rooted in a Christian understanding of the world. Consequently, some readers may disagree with much or all of what I write, and will find this preface worst of all. It will seem drivel not worth another second of their time as a modern person, and they are right. I would caution such a "modern thinker" to read no further, because they will find no enjoyment in this novel, except perhaps a sort of cynical, self-satisfied feeling of superiority to one who still holds such beliefs.

To those still with me, allow me to explain the impetus behind this short work. Most immediate of all was the desire to write something and to write it quickly; I began this novel as part of National Novel Writing Month and completed the thirty-day challenge of 50,000 words in 23 days.

Yet deeper than this was the seed of longing, implanted in me some time during childhood, to write a story that made me feel what all the tales I loved as a boy had made me feel: namely, a sense of wonder, adventure, exploration, discovery, danger and ultimately a solid ending (not necessarily a happy one, merely a firm finish).

The story grew from this seed, this wish to write a simple story-driven novel I myself would have enjoyed as a boy, and it grew very quickly without direction, because I was racing against a self-imposed deadline. It was a quest story with only vague starting directions that proceeded with reckless speed. There was no outline, no grand design that I followed. Consequently I should not be at all surprised that it turned out the way it did.

I had perilously opened myself up to direction from God. Should I have been surprised that He was all too willing to lead me?

C.S. Lewis used the term "Joy" for that unexplainable sensation of which men sometimes have flickering ephemeral glimpses, but which disappears as soon as one contemplates it. In *Lud-in-the-Mist* by Hope Mirrlees, the mayor Chanticleer shudders at the sound of the "Note," that shattering intrusion of Faerie music into his mundane conventionality. To such ideas, and some extent, to the wanderings of William Morris' young prince Ralph in *The Well at the World's End*, my tale of the boy Fritz is deeply indebted. I have also borrowed some place names from Morris.

When I first began writing this book, I did not intend to write any sort of allegorical story, much less a sort of "spiritual allegory," and still least of all, that most sentimental of writing and most despised form of the modern world: a Christian story. This is not to say I saw no value in reading such a story; *the Chronicles of Narnia* thrilled me as a child and the Joy that I found there has never left me.

I simply never imagined or even particularly wanted to *write* one of those stories myself (a story with a deeper meaning)—even when I found myself far along in the process of writing one! Perhaps I was prejudiced in this respect, because of countless literature classes in which the "deeper meaning" had to be parsed out of the writing while the ecstasy, the adventure and the simple pleasure of the story itself was ignored — or killed — in the incessant dissection. This is something like taking a plate of world-class fare from a top chef, tearing the cuisine apart with fork and knife to try to identify the ingredients, smashing and scattering the food all over the plate, and then leaving without ever taking a bite and tasting!

It was from fear of this, of producing a story that could only be read with a *wink, wink, nudge, nudge* by tedious literature teachers, and not for the simple enjoyment of the tale, that I was reluctant to even acknowledge that halfway through the writing some semblance of allegory was, in fact, beginning to show through. I ignored it; I shook my head like a stubborn child and said, "Nuh uh, I did not do that."

Then, I realized that what I had done was only natural. That as a Christian, I could no more produce a non-Christian work of art than I as a human being could lay the egg of a hen. To attempt to do so was to run away from the Son only to run into the Father; or ignore them both because I was drawing closer to the Holy Spirit. Wherever I turned, there He was. How could I ever, or why would I even *want* to, produce a story with no deeper meaning? Why write at all, if not to glorify the values and morals I hold dear and by extension, to glorify the Lord who gave us those values?

Yet I must insist, although this tale is allocorical, that you do not pick it apart to try to identify each individual element or symbol. Such guesswork kills the spirit of the writing. Read the book as a whole and feel the soul of it. Do not single out the ingredients; enjoy the meal.

A word about the book's spirit: I have long been afflicted with a serious case of wanderlust, or perhaps more broadly of *Sehnsucht*. Allow me for the last time to mention C.S. Lewis, because he defined this as:

> "That unnameable something, desire for which pierces us like a rapier at the smell of bonfire, the sound of wild ducks flying overhead, the title of The Well at the World's End, the opening lines of 'Kubla Khan', the morning cobwebs in late summer, or the noise of falling waves."

A certain painting in my parent's house has always pierced me so. And it was from this lifelong affliction that the restless Fritz was born. In this sense, Fritz is an advanced version of my own childhood imagination personified in the form of a character. It is that ineffable desire, that *Sehnsucht*, which first pierces the boy Fritz at the sight of the harvest moon and which draws him forward into all the events of the novel.

Without understanding this feeling, there is nothing at all to this novel.

Now I may not have produced a very good work of art, but I hope that, after all, it is Good. That is to say, I hope the values and ideals point toward the Ultimate Good in the Universe, the Triune God of Christianity, the Light by which we all see.

— R.W. Schmidt, November 2013

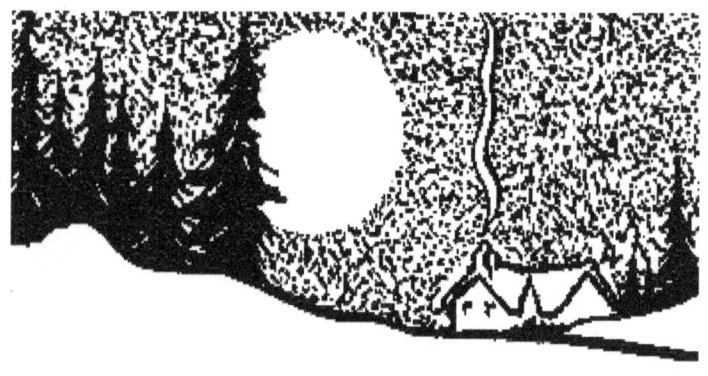

Chapter 1

Many years ago, in a time before your ancestors were young men, on a night when the first crisp tendrils of autumn were just beginning to encircle the great trunks of the wild wood, a little boy named Fritz lay awake in his bed.

Fritz could not sleep because the beams of the harvest moon flickered in through the windows and filled the little cottage that he shared with his mother and his father, and those beams gave such light as to make it almost day in that place. But it was not day; it was well past midnight, so late that the little boy knew Father would surely punish him if Fritz were to get up out of bed.

Yet this is an intolerable situation to be in as a nine-year-old boy, with the pale moon shining in upon your sleepless eyes and the sound of rolling thunder away off in the slumbering night and the shivering rustle of the trees in the wood far afield like a beckoning whisper. Fritz lay fighting against his boyish nature for a long time, that gnawing restlessness that all boys and all men who were once boys will know well, but he could never have won that battle, so that at last, he put one foot out on the cold dirt floor and then the other one.

With quiet, practiced movements, the little shadow of the boy flitted around the room and slipped on his leather shoes and donned a wolf's skin coat. Nimble fingers opened the cupboard door without a squeak of its iron hinges and gathered a few provisions from within. He took such as he felt necessary for his modest, midnight journey: bread, a small block of cheese, a couple of sausages that Father had made recently. And because he was already on a criminal endeavor, he also took the three frosted scones that Mother had baked that day.

All of this he wrapped in a neat bundle, stuffed into a knapsack, and slung this knapsack over his shoulder, and when he had done this, he also fastened a worn sheath to his belt with a leather strip. Inside this sheath was a finely honed knife that Father had given him for his birthday. Some boys, whose own fevered stirrings of the heart have been twisted, may turn such knifes upon the weak, upon birds and squirrels that come within their reach, but kind-hearted Fritz could never have even imagined such a thing. He had used his knife many times for carving and cutting and chopping, but never, never for killing a living thing. Yet he knew what other creatures besides birds and squirrels lived in the wild wood, and he did not wish to be defenseless.

And so, girded thus, young Fritz crept on light toes to the door of the cottage, eased it open and slipped out into the cool darkness.

In front of the cottage ran a short walkway, bordered on either side by Mother's flowerbeds, overfilled with many-colored plants and flowers that created such dazzling images as to rival rainbows when the sun's light played in the petals. But now beneath the moon, the flowers shimmered with an unearthly quality in colors without names, so that Fritz had to rub his eyes and look twice and wonder whether he was in waking life or in a dream.

Yet it made no difference.

He cast his eyes upward and away to the harvest moon, to that great, gray-orange orb that floated low on the distant horizon, and the boy smiled and shrugged because he was well-provisioned, well-armed and well beyond caring.

With a gentle skip, he bounded noiselessly down the front walk, away beyond the limits of the encircling fence, then down and through an overgrown ditch and up to the other side where a fallow field stretched for nearly half a mile to the edge of the woodlands. Over the unplowed earth of this empty field hovered a dense mist, so thick that Fritz could barely discern the dark shapes of the countless trees of the wood beyond. There was no sound, none but the whisper of the night's deep, and a little boy's footfalls on the cool autumn earth.

The world was wrapped in beautiful loneliness.

Fritz hurried on through the mists of the moon, drawn ever forward by a child's sense of wonder into a world that promised many and varied marvels, such that the simple cottage of his parents and their farm could not hope to match.

As he ventured farther into the field, the mist thickened so that very quickly Fritz lost sight of the farm behind him. All that remained were the looming trunks of the forest before him, gradually taking shape as he approached them. Higher and higher they rose into the dome of night overhead. But when Fritz came to the forest's very edge, he turned back to look across the field, and through a quick parting of the mist, he had a last fleeting glimpse of his family's cottage silhouetted by the light of the moon against a backdrop of rolling pastures and farmland and scattered groves of trees.

Then Fritz turned and stepped into the wild wood.

Dried pine needles crunched under his feet and their fragrance floated up from the forest floor to surround him with gentle comfort. He found the well-trodden path easily, even in the darkness, and he followed its narrow, winding way through the maze of trees. He clutched his

4

knapsack to his shoulder and tramped through the scattered undergrowth. He was not far now from his destination, and his heart was light and cheerful despite the late hour; for how could a boy so young and full of life not be cheerful to be free in the wilderness?

Ahead of him in the shadows, Fritz spied the Great Oak, its trunk as large around as a house, a tree of the ancient days that served as a landmark in this tangled wood. He hastened toward it, for now he knew for certain that he drew near to his own place, his secret place. As Fritz passed the Great Oak, he reached out and rubbed its primal bark and felt the cool roughness of this silent watcher, and when he did this, the branches shook and the leaves shivered and many of them fell softly around the little boy.

Fritz laughed, and he caught one of these leaves and placed it in his knapsack with all of his other belongings, because it seemed to be a gift from the Great Oak.

Then he was off again, scurrying down the path into the unknown marvels of the autumn night. Some steps farther down the path, Fritz descended through a screen of ash saplings that grew close upon each other. When he pushed through these, he saw the serpentine line of a trickling brook, snaking its hazy way through the lonely wood. He smiled as he bounded down the sloped bank and splashed into the cool shallows.

The water of the tiny river sprayed up as he crashed through it and up the opposite bank.

When the child had passed on into the night, the brook, briefly disturbed, returned patiently to its gurgling softness, rolling away into the far away deep somewhere.

But Fritz gave that brook no more thought, because he had a boy's mind, nimble and ever leaping from this to that, for there is so much to be seen in this world, far too much to linger on things behind. A boy's mind may only ever consider what a boy's eyes see at any one moment. And at that very moment, this boy's eyes saw what he had been seeking this night.

Fritz had arrived at his secret place.

None alive knew of it, no living man, except for him. He had discovered it and kept it, and no man had set foot here that he knew of. He guarded the knowledge of this place in the profound secrecy of a child's heart, because he wished it to be so, because even a child knows that there are few things of more value in this world than a place of solitary refuge.

So Fritz loved and cherished this place, and stole away here when he needed to enjoy time in the company of his own heart.

The place was shaped in a perfect circle, a clearing in the midst of the wood, a round space of ankle-high grass in the green center of which stood a stone pillar about twice the height of

Fritz. And upon this obelisk were carved many deep marks that joined together to make a strange writing of a kind that Fritz had never seen elsewhere. Chunks of the stone were missing in places so that the boy knew it was an ancient thing, more ancient even than the Great Oak, beaten and worn by the turning of countless seasons. Man or beast or some Thing else perhaps had fashioned it and placed it here, but who could now tell of its origins lost somewhere in the blank waste of the past?

The stone was not of this age, but of an age long lost—long, long ago, before patient Night had grown weary and dark, when the moon was as young and fair as a tender maiden.

Fritz touched the pillar this night as one embraces a sorely missed friend after many days apart. Then, he sighed and sat on the spongy grass with his legs crossed and placed his knapsack on his knees and flung open the flap of it. He took the bread and cheese and the couple of sausages and began to prepare for himself a humble banquet in the light of the watching moon.

This had been his aim after all, just a simple meal in the solitude of his secret place.

Something in this meadow and places like it, humble and hidden, offers respite and moments of calm for the wild, adventurous soul that plagues the boys of the world, the wanderer's soul that gnaws and aches inside of them even unto gray manhood. It is the plague of horizons, the plague of the next river bend, the plague that drives men over the vast oceans into strange lands beyond the edges of the maps.

Some get it worse than others, and Fritz had it worse than any.

Yet every time he sat alone and quiet in this place at the foot of the weird obelisk, he had a moment of relief from that tugging of his soul. He was able to sit and enjoy the peace of a stilled heart and mind.

So it was that he ate his meal that night, munching on the bread and cheese and sausages until he had had his fill.

But he did not eat the three sweet scones that he had stolen from Mother's pantry. These he left untouched in his knapsack and saved them as if they were things of great worth, for to Fritz they were.

When he finished eating, he fell backward into the yielding hug of the meadow grass and lay staring at the distant stars twinkling in that mysterious sky. The seconds danced away through the whispering leaves of the wood, and somewhere they turned into long minutes and began to put down the roots of lingering hours.

Sometime later, Fritz was about to pull himself up and pry himself away from that place, because he did not wish to be caught out of doors by

Father tonight. Yet how he loved his secret place! Thus, he was wrestling with his mind when he heard the sound.

It thundered and crashed through the trees like a sudden storm falling upon him. The clear spiteful noise bit into his heart.

A wolf was howling at the harvest moon.

The call rose mournfully into the dark, and was taken up by another, and then another, and another, and so on until the wild wood echoed from every direction with the rise and fall of the wailing animals.

Fritz was surrounded by the beasts of the night.

He stood suddenly, frightened, and looked about the meadow that had seemed so sweet moments before, and saw around its fringes many yellow pairs of eyes amongst the trees.

Another lone howl went up and the chorus followed it; now baying, now yelping, now yipping in short, clipped noises that seemed like hateful laughter.

The relief that Fritz had felt earlier fled immediately at this sight and his adventurous soul flooded back in upon him, so quickly that it smothered the tiny flame of fear. He drew his knife and held it before him as another round of yelping and yipping erupted in the darkness.

A wolf leapt into the clearing, its teeth bared and its face contorted into a mask of ravenous death. Fritz faced it defiantly with his little knife.

When the wolf pounced, Fritz slashed at it and cut deeply into the fur of the beast. If it had been just this one-on-one battle, the boy would surely have triumphed.

But the two warriors were joined by the rest of the wolf pack, one after another, as they bounded into the fray on the mead. Fritz would have been quickly overrun by the wolves, and he knew at once that his only chance was to run.

So run he did.

Fritz saw an opening in the hedge of razor-teeth and dashed through it and away into the wood. The animals barked and snapped and were close behind.

Fritz headed in the opposite direction of the farm because he thought he could lose the wolves in the wood and because he did not want to lead these ravenous beasts to the cottage to devour him there along with Mother and Father. He ran and ran, and soon he found that he ran due west toward the harvest moon, which hung on the horizon before him, seeming to rest upon the ridges of the western mountains.

Deeper into the wood he ran, until he was under trees that he had never seen before, trees with gnarled trunks, with limbs that were draped heavily with hanging moss. Still he ran, because the wolves had not slackened their pace, nor had they lessened in their hunger. Their jaws chomped and tore at the air as they tried to devour the little boy.

But ever were the boy's heels just out of reach as he tore through the tangled thickets. Oh, how the wolves snarled and ripped at the cool night air, but never did their teeth touch Fritz.

He was as much at home in that midnight wood as those savage creatures, for the blood of the forest folk pumped hard in the boy's veins and gave strength to his spindly legs and sure feet. Never did his toes catch an errant vine or twisted root, but they flew over the uneven ground as easily as if it were a worn cart path.

In fact, so refreshed and strengthened had Fritz been by his visit to the mysterious obelisk that in no time, he was leaving the wolves behind in the deepening darkness. Ahead loomed the jagged peaks of the mountain wall and the moon perched precariously on high. Yet Fritz, as energetic and light-footed as he was, could not keep up this pace forever. He began to lag, and though he kept a safe distance between himself and the wolves, still they stayed in sight.

After much twisting and weaving through the wild wood, Fritz was almost spent. Again, he heard the growling and the slobbering mouths of the creatures just behind him.

He had just reached the top of a small rise, or hillock, and below he could see the misty path of a small river or brook that he assumed was the very same that he had crossed earlier. Yet if he had had any real time to consider this (the wolves being mere feet away by then) Fritz might have realized that this could not at all be the same brook.

For one thing, he had been running westward all the time in his flight from the wolves, and so with every step drawing nearer to the menacing mountains. And for another, this stream upon which he now gazed was so unearthly strange that surely no mortal boy had ever looked upon its waters before.

Later, Fritz might have described the strange river like this:

Its course cut a twisting line like a vivid wound across the expanse of land between the forest and the first of the rocky foothills of the mountains. Neither tree nor reed grew upon its banks, and the reason for this must have been that the banks were constantly shifting. For even now Fritz saw that the stream wiggled and writhed back and forth. The crooks and bends, and the little eddies and pools formed in them were inconstant; if one looked with enough intensity, one saw that the little rivulet squirmed as if alive.

And the waters of this stream were of such a singular quality that struck man and beast dumb before them. Those waters had not the look of a nighttime brook; they showed not the shimmering blackness of water under moonlight.

They were not reflective at all really, though they did shine with a mystifying light. But the shine was as of its own source, not the reflection of some other luminous body, but as if the river itself glowed and twinkled. The stream sent forth its own rays, and its surface gleamed brightly in the inky night.

The waters shone pure white.

The flowing stream looked like a long dancing swath of silk or gossamer caught in the wind, or like a giant bowl of milk that had been spilt over the earth.

Again, this is how the boy Fritz might have described it later.

At that very moment, his descriptive powers were severely hindered by the proximity of such deadly animals.

The wolves were almost upon him!

Taking a deep breath, Fritz leapt over the side of the hillock and tumbled down the embankment toward the uncanny river. When he came to his feet, he saw that the wolves had not followed but had stopped short at the summit of the hill. The creatures howled and growled and snarled for the lost meal, but were unwilling to descend or to come any nearer to that white water.

For his part, Fritz kept running headlong into those strange shallows, not trusting the dire beasts behind to give up so easily. Floundering and splashing and making much noise, the little boy swam across the river and flopped, cold and wet, on the far shore.

Chapter 2

As Fritz stumbled up the far bank and shivered in the moonlight, he looked around himself in astonishment. All throughout his flight from the wolves, he had kept the western mountains directly in front of him, and he could see just over their rugged shoulders that great gray-orange shape of the moon floating in the blackness.

Now he looked up at those high craggy peaks so close to him and saw no moon at all. But looking back eastward, over that strange river, he saw, larger than he had ever seen in his life, the imposing face of the moon staring back at him. The lunar circle filled the sky, so that it blocked out the twinkling stars. Neither the wolves nor the hillock that he had tumbled down could be seen, but only this overpowering image of the harvest moon.

As he pondered this sudden change, he muttered to himself, "How did that get there?"

And to his great surprise, a voice answered with:

"Oh, but the question should be, how did *you* get *here*?"

Fritz looked all around him, but saw no speaker for this voice. Long seconds passed in silence, except for the trickling of the white stream.

"Who said that?" asked Fritz, "Where are you?"

"I am *here*, and so are you. And so I repeat my question: how did you get here?"

"I swam," said Fritz to the invisible speaker, giving little thought to how very strange this was. "Simple as that."

"Simple as that, he says!" came the reply, followed by a light chuckling that flitted and danced around him as easily as leaves in a fall breeze. "But it is precisely *not* that simple, boy, or all would do it. No, it isn't simple at all to come *here*."

"And just where is here?" said the boy, who by now was turning in circles and beginning to feel quite impatient with the faceless voice.

"Hallo, I say, where is *here*?"

"Why, you've crossed the border into the Lands Beyond the Moon."

"I have?" said Fritz in bewilderment, staring back at the moon in the eastern sky, "But I tell you all I did was swim that little stream there."

For a fleeting second, Fritz thought he heard a sharp gasp around him, but then he realized that it must have just been the wind whipping down out of the rocky mountains nearby.

The invisible speaker said, "Truly, you swam that river?"

"Yes!"

Jumbled whispers broke out in the air all around him, as if a great assembly were debating this fact. But after a few moments, the drifting chorus of voices mingled all together until there seemed to be only one speaker arguing with himself. As the faint discourse drifted away, that single voice spoke aloud again:

"How can it be that a human enters those waters and yet lives?"

Fritz shook his head, white droplets flicking from his damp hair, and shrugged.

"I don't know. What waters are they? I mean, does this stream have a name?"

"A name? Why, it has many names! But I think the one that you would be most familiar with is that name in your own tongue. For I believe your people call it the Milky Way."

"The Milky Way is not a river!" said Fritz, chuckling with all the smugness of a little boy pointing out the mistakes of others.

"Oh, but it is."

Fritz turned to the strange stream, its glow now even brighter, and said, "But the Milky Way is in the sky. It's a path of stars…"

"A river of stars," corrected the voice, "Flowing waters of starlight."

"Stars?" said Fritz numbly, "But...but then, how did I cross it?"

"Ah ha! My question exactly," said the voice, "Few living do."

"Then, have I...I mean, am I—"

"Oh, no, child! You are still very much alive! Though I may say, not as Alive as you might be if you had died."

Fritz rubbed his damp head in puzzlement at this. The voice seemed only to speak in riddles.

"Who are you?" said the little boy, "And why can I not see you?"

"I am the Watcher in the Wind," said the voice, "And as to why you cannot see, well that is easily answered. No being, human or otherwise, can see if their eyes are closed!"

"But my eyes aren't...what sort of being are you?" said Fritz, wishing he could see the thing he addressed, "I mean, are you good or bad?"

"I am not sure how to answer that," said the voice, "Certainly I wish you no evil, and so cannot be called bad, if that is what you meant. And yet, my ways are not the ways of Man, and so I do not know if I am what you mean by good, though I am of the most incomprehensible Good in the Universe."

"Well, that is not a very clear answer," mumbled Fritz to himself.

"But I am not a very clear thing, not yet to you, at least," said the Watcher, "I am a Mystery, and you may come to know me in time, yet I lose none of my Mysteriousness. Your eyes will be opened One Day, and then you will not need to see, because you will *know*. Blessed are they that have not seen. You do not need to see the wind to know it. And I am the First Wind—which moved upon the face of the waters."

"Oh," said Fritz, not at all understanding really. He was still having trouble coming to terms with a disembodied voice. Yet the little boy guessed that if he could accept that such a voice existed, then he could accept that its nature was mysterious. Still he naturally had questions.

"What exactly do you do?"

"Do? I do everything, and yet I allow all to be done without my force. I compel all, while compelling none. I am within and without. I do without doing. I make all things new, yet unmake nothing old. And of course, I watch!"

Fritz felt more confused than ever and said, "Yes, I gathered that from your name. But what do you watch?"

"Everything."

"Well, *why* do you watch?"

"Why?" repeated the Watcher in a tone like confusion. "I watch to See."

Fritz's voice was becoming exasperated as he said, "Of course you watch to see. But what is the reason behind it? Do you report to someone what you see, or do you just watch for your own sake?

You see, back home at the gates of the great cities, we have guards, and these men watch out along the walls to protect the cities from dangers outside. And they report to the mayor or master."

"Hmm," considered the Watcher, with a sound like a chilled breeze down a chimney, "That sounds reasonable enough. But why should I do that here? Very few ever cross the Milky Way, so I have little to guard against. And you do not seem like much danger to me. And as I do not wish to keep anyone out—for the door is open to all who knock—I think I would make a rather terrible guard."

Fritz nodded in agreement and said, "Very terrible."

The Watcher in the Wind laughed and said, "This is good fortune for you, for I am not a guard, but a Comforter. And as I know you, and have always known you, since before you ever were born, I know that you will want to go farther on in the Lands Beyond the Moon. I know what calls you there. And because I am no guard, I will not hinder you on your way."

"But how do you know…" said Fritz, almost in a daze at the Watcher's words, "And how can I go on? How can I cross those mountains?"

"Now you have asked the Watcher the right question! I can help you there, for I have been watching since before the Milky Way first began its eternal trickling. Go on the path that you will find up this rise, and follow it up through the foothills. Farther on, you will find a pass through the mountains called the Way of Silence, and to reach it along the path, remember this: *keep to the right*. You will come to many forks and might have to make decisions along the way, but never forget: keep to the right!"

"I won't forget," said Fritz, already beginning to trot away to the West, "Thank you."

Behind him, the Watcher in the Wind said, "Keep to the right! That would be something to remember even after the pass. Keep to the right!"

"Keep to the right," Fritz repeated to himself, "That should be easy enough."

But Fritz would soon learn a lesson that it takes grown men many years to learn sometimes.

It is not always easy to keep to the right.

Chapter 3

Up and up the small rise ran Fritz, and gradually the foliage began to grow around him again. The farther he ran from the Milky Way, the more wild growth appeared on the foothills. Here and there were copses of trees, growing close together like a weary group of travelers bundled together for warmth in the shadow of the mountains. Wild shrubs grew in patches on the rolling land. Wildflowers bloomed despite the chilly fall weather. As Fritz passed these colorful blooms, he wondered what power let them flourish at so late and so cold a time of the year.

At the top of the far riverbank, where three tall swishing cottonwoods grew like sentries upon a rampart, Fritz found the start of the path, of which the Watcher had spoken. An arch of stone, like an entry gate to the Lands Beyond the Moon, marked the start of the path. To Fritz, it looked like a door in an invisible wall. He was just about to pass under it, when he noticed something even odder.

The stone arch was carved with the same ancient runes as that standing stone back in the wild wood. The deep etchings bore an uncanny likeness to those other familiar marks that the little boy had spent so much time wondering at. Could it be that those same men, or beings, who built this arch had also placed the standing stone in the forest? Had others, thousands and thousands of years ago, walked this same path under the moon's pale glow?

Fritz wished that he could ask the Watcher in the Wind these things, but somehow he knew that even if he walked back down to the starry river, he would not find the Watcher there. The night wind from the mountains was too swift for that being to stay long. So Fritz put his hand on the cold, rough stone and passed beneath the arch without a word.

On the other side, the ground underfoot became suddenly smooth, as smooth as the packed earthen floor of Father's barn. It felt so smooth, in fact, that Fritz thought that if he ran a horse cart over it, he could sit in the driver's seat without feeling a single jostle or jolt.

As it was, he had no such cart. So, shouldering his small knapsack, which still contained the Great Oak leaf and Mother's scones that had somehow escaped the sogginess of the river Milky Way, Fritz set off at a brisk pace up the path of the foothills.

"This isn't so bad," he said to himself.

And it wasn't.

The mountain air, though chilly, was brisk and refreshing like a cold draught of water after a long day's work. Fritz inhaled deeply and greedily, jaunting over the path as easily and carefree as a cloud soars through the sky. In some places the forest growth was rather thick, as dense as any thicket in the wild wood, and this only made Fritz wonder all the more at those bare banks around the starry river.

But a boyish shrug was enough to dismiss these wonderings, and soon Fritz was almost jogging uphill with satisfied ease. Even the frightful thought of wolves disappeared from his happy mind. He did have one last fleeting worry of Father and Mother and the farm and home, and that very strange dislocation of the moon, but even these thoughts were soon gone as he walked the path.

Before long, the foothills turned rockier and began their gradual change from hills to mountains. Fritz had to slow his pace as boulders began to appear in the road, as if tossed there by some powerful and angry fiend from on high. Ahead of him, the summits of the mountains were lost in the clouds. Still Fritz walked on, certain that the summits were up there and would wait patiently on him, even if those dense clouds blocked them from sight just now. He shivered at the thought of having to climb one of those mountain peaks to cross over the range and was very thankful that the Watcher had told him of the pass called the Way of Silence.

The first fork in the path was just beyond a fallen elm tree. Fritz stopped for a moment, and sat on the fallen log to survey the two roads. Of course, he remembered the Watcher's repeated advice.

A jumble of stones almost blocked the whole left side of the fork where they had fallen from the cliffs. This mass of granite and limestone would have made it awfully difficult to take that way. What's more, the chilled air that floated down that side brought with it a rank smell, a smell like rotten meat, like some dead animal left too long exposed to the elements. Fritz wrinkled up his nose at it and held his breath.

Yet the right side of the fork continued on much like the path that Fritz had been walking so far. A few bunches of wildflowers grew there, strewn over the rise like confetti, pinks and purples and bright yellows, and bunches of welcoming columbine, wafting their sweet smell to him on the autumn air. Not a single obstacle blocked that way as far as the little boy could see.

"Keep to the right!" had been the Watcher's words.

"Why, you would have to be a fool to not keep to the right!" said Fritz from his seat on the fallen elm.

He was right, of course, but more right than he knew at that moment.

He hopped to his feet and half-walked, half-skipped up the right side of the fork. Eventually the smoothness of the road turned a bit bumpier, a bit harder to walk, but not much. It remained an easy stroll, especially considering how steep the path became as it wound its way ever higher into the twisting labyrinth of the mountains.

Fritz soon became aware of two other changes as he walked. The first that he noticed were the wildflowers dwindling away as he walked. In their stead grew scraggly mountain grasses and lichen coatings on the fallen stones.

The second change was more noticeable. The path took a sudden curve into a sort of gorge or ravine, so that the walls of stone began to creep in on him, closing in on either side high above. Closer and closer they came until Fritz felt like he was walking down an enormous hallway. Indeed, as he walked, the boy pretended that he *was* in a hallway, a great gilded corridor, and that he was entering the hall of some giant-king of the mountains. To fit this scene, he walked with the noble bearing of a knight come to pay tribute to his liege lord: straight-backed, head held high, chest puffed out gallantly. The only things that he lacked were a fitting steed to ride and a shield or banner of some kind to display his heraldry.

So, stooping, he picked up a long and sturdy stick that lay by the path side, about the size of a shepherd's staff, and tied his knapsack to the end of it, and lifted it high overhead, as if to make a symbol of his house to signal his approach to his lord's hall.

He even began to hum a bold melody as if he had just told his faithful squire to strike up a tune as they marched. The little boy tramped like this through the shadow of the ravine walls, humming along as his knapsack bounced in the air above him, a knight with no horse and no worries.

Soon the young knight came to another fork in the road and stood for a moment, marching in place. Then, he said:

"Forward, men."

And with this order given to his imaginary companions, he took the right fork as the Watcher had instructed. As he walked away, he could not help noticing that at this fork, the road left had looked smoother and not so steep. But he gave this little thought, soon engrossed again in his knightly game.

He hummed even louder as he came at last out of the ravine and the world opened up around him. He felt a joyous sense of being alive, almost like victory, but not quite, as he stared out over the vast landscape below him, spread out like some beautiful tapestry depicting a dreamy night. But this landscape was real, dotted with groves of swaying trees and festooned with the blue ribbons of small tributaries flowing down into the east. Even herds of grazing animals could be seen below. From this height, Fritz could not make out what sort of animals they were exactly, but what did it matter?

Fritz struck up the tune again, joined now by an imaginary band of minstrels to play the music and an imaginary troupe of maiden dancers, all of them merrily celebrating the March of Fritz.

The little boy was so enraptured by his song, so caught up in the heady brew of nobility and fame, that he did not notice the caves that began to show their mouths in the rock wall beside him. The path twisted back into the deep of the mountains and lost the wide landscape behind him. But the rock face to his right soon grew full of clefts and yawning caves. In this odd place, any number of strange creatures might have been hidden within, but the marching boy took no notice.

Not until the sound of falling pebbles met his ear, loud enough to break through the rowdy tune he hummed. Fritz stopped in the path, suddenly aware of how dark and cold it was in these mountains. Another noise came from inside the cave a few feet away on his right, a sound like feet scampering toward him. More stones and pebbles fell, bouncing and skittering out of the cave and falling away down the steep path. When the sound of growling started in the mouth of the cave and two little points of light like eyes peered out of the darkness, Fritz had a fleeting wish that he had never gotten out of his bed at the farm.

Before the boy could react, the creature leapt from the cave, flying in a flash of fur over Fritz's head. As the animal passed, the little boy felt its hot breath near his neck and smelled its heavy musk on the crisp air.

When the paws of the creature came down on the other side of him, Fritz turned, ready to fight for his life with the sturdy stick in his hand. Then, he saw that the creature was a red fox, smaller than any dog that Fritz had ever seen. Yet, for all its smallness, the animal still bared sharp teeth in the pale moonlight.

"Shh," whispered Fritz, lowering the stick and extending a friendly hand to try to calm the animal.

"Do not shush me," said the fox, its words mingled with a growl. Fritz started and pulled back in surprise, though he shouldn't have been too surprised to find a talking fox after already encountering a bodiless voice this same night.

"I'm sorry," said Fritz.

"As you should be," said the fox, his teeth still flashing fiercely, "What do you mean, parading through here, making so much noise in the middle of the night while decent animals are trying to sleep? Do you want to wake the Shadows?"

"Shadows?"

"Keep your voice down," snarled the fox. Then, motioning with his sleek head into the cave, he added, "Go on, get inside. Quickly."

The fox's voice was so insistent and contained just enough fear that Fritz ducked his head under the entrance to the cave and followed without a second thought. The cave was bare and dark, but deeper than it had seemed from the outside. Fritz could not see the back of it, lost as it was in the heavy dark. Behind him, the fox cast his gaze one last time up and down the mountain path.

"Go on, go on," said the little red creature, nudging the boy with his cold nose, "Do not linger on the threshold, boy. Go in!"

Fritz felt confused as to how he should act in the den of a fox, never having been in one before. He stepped carefully into the deeper darkness of the cave and discovered there a small door, closed fast. He stopped in front of it, baffled by the beautiful woodwork flourishes around the graceful golden handle.

"Open it," said the fox, "It's not locked."

Fritz did as he was told, and the door swung in easily enough. At once, the candlelight and the glow of a warm hearth burst forth to greet him.

He and the fox entered a rich den, fit enough for the wealthiest merchant of the burgs. But this den belonged to a fox, and the luxury of its furnishing seemed odd considering what lay just outside the front door.

"What is this place?" asked Fritz.

"My home, silly boy," said the fox, as he hopped gracefully into a velvet chair just in front of the hearthfire, turned about twice, and plopped down on its soft cushion. "Why do you think I brought you in here?"

"I thought it was to get away from the, uh," said Fritz, trying to remember, "The Shadows..."

"It was," said the fox, his eyes suddenly narrowing, "But just because those vile things are without doesn't mean I cannot be a welcoming host to a weary traveler."

Now the fox softened his gaze, but looked the little boy up and down, examining him closely with shining eyes.

"You *are* an interesting traveler."

"Thank you," said Fritz, bowing slightly, still wondering about the manners one should show while in a fox's den.

"I am heading for the pass."

"The pass?" said the fox in wonderment, "The Way of Silence? You mean to go through the mountains. Into the beyond. What draws you that way?"

"There is something…something…," said Fritz, grasping for some word to explain that longing within him, that feeling that even he did not understand, that fleeting horizon in his soul that he must chase after or die.

But there was no word.

And the fox seemed to understand, for there passed a moment between them as they shared a solemn silence in the presence of that timeless melancholy. Then, the fox smiled wistfully at the little boy.

"It is that, then."

"Yes."

"Then, you mustn't stop here," said the fox, "And you mustn't go back home. Not yet anyway."

"You mean I have to leave?" said Fritz, thinking unpleasantly about the cold mountain path and that word, Shadow, which the fox had said so frightfully.

"Oh, no, I am not kicking you out," said the fox with a quick shake of his head, "I only meant that you cannot give up. Do not misunderstand me. You are most welcome here."

"Thank you, um…I'm sorry. I don't know your name."

The fox's eyes twinkled with friendliness and mischief as he said, "You may call me Florian." Here the animal bowed his head and added, "At your service."

"And I am Fritz. At yours."

The two fell to talking then as though they were the oldest of friends, as if there had never been a day when they did not know each other. As two kindred spirits suddenly reunited, each found his compliment in the other. How easy it is to make such a friend when you are young, and you give your heart freely. So it was with Fritz, who in the sudden kindling fire of their new friendship, gave his heart to the fox, and the fox, his to Fritz.

The hearthfire popped and crackled soothingly and its fragrant smokiness reminded Fritz of Mother's kitchen in the cottage back home. The warmth of the fox's den wrapped around him like a freshly laundered blanket and quickly made him forget about the chilled winds without. Yet no matter how comfortable he was here, the little boy could not forget the fear that he had heard in the fox's voice.

"Pardons, Florian, but who…or what…are the Shadows?"

The fox's eyes narrowed again. He seemed unwilling to answer at first, continuing simply to stare into the fire meditatively. For long, quiet moments, only the soft sizzle of burning wood filled the den. Finally the animal spoke:

"This is not a conversation that we should have so deep in the night. Nevertheless…"

The fox paused and then added, "Can I get you coffee? If we are to stay up late discussing unpleasantness, I think you will need it."

"Sure," said Fritz, as he found a seat on a soft easy chair near the fire, but not too near. The glowing warmth pierced his every bone and relaxed his aching toes.

The young boy had never tasted coffee before, though Father occasionally drank a cup of the strongly scented drink. Soon, a steaming cup of brown liquid sat in front of him on a saucer, and Fritz could not have said how it got there. He had not seen the fox carry it to him, but then again, he had not been paying much attention, but staring idly into the hearthfire.

"Thank you," he said, taking the cup and sniffing at its contents. The drink smelled intoxicating and tasted even better. In seconds, the boy perked up and felt even more anxious to know the answer to his earlier question.

The fox, however, seemed no more eager to talk of the matter now, even though he and his guest were quite comfortable. Fritz had to bring up the subject again.

"Well," he said, "The Shadows?"

The fox spoke as one who finds the words distasteful.

"The Shadows are horrific beasts who dwell in the deepest, darkest places of the mountains' black heart, and of whom it is best to say as little as possible. I will tell you only this, and then please, I want you to never ask me about them again. There were some in these ancient mountains who once worshiped the Shadows, but no longer."

"Why?" whispered Fritz.

"The Shadows ate them."

Fritz recoiled in the chair, pulling away from the blunt and terrifying words that hung in the air like a black cloud. He shook his head in horror and disbelief. The fox continued:

"The Shadows desire only to spread their wickedness and to consume good hearts."

"But they don't actually…"

"Oh, yes," said Florian, gravely, "If the Shadows had found you alone on the path, they would have fallen upon your heart as well."

Fritz took a long, soothing sip of the coffee and shivered despite the hearthfire's warmth. When he swallowed the drink, he said:

"What do they look like?"

"You should not ask. I have never seen them," said Florian, "And I do not wish to. Neither should you. Yet I have heard tales of their look, though I will not share these tales with you. Such things are too terrifying to consider, even in the safety of one's own home before a crackling fire. Let us speak no more of them this night."

Something in the way the fox said this last sentence made Fritz not even consider asking again. In truth, he did not care to learn more of such creatures; what little he had heard of the Shadows was enough to place the hot iron of terror in the pit of his stomach.

He watched the fire again and sighed, thinking of how close he had been to danger and death, and how completely unseen it had been to him. Fritz had been oblivious to anything but his joyous, song-filled marching, the glee of boyish freedom. And now the horror and fear of these beasts had stolen that sweetness from him. The enticing honey of contentment turned bitter on his lips.

Fritz would not let it remain so.

The lure of the mountain pass crept back into his soul, the hunger of that appetite that he could not satisfy. He had to go on, to walk through the pass and into the beyond.

"I cannot stay longer," the little boy said to the fox, "Though lurking death be out there, I have to go on."

"I know."

There was no need to explain why, no need to try to put into words the 'groanings which cannot be uttered,' for the fox had felt the same way as a kit so long ago.

And now he felt it again, felt it as a dam burst within him.

"I will go with you," said Florian to Fritz.

Chapter 4

"Oh, I would very much like a companion!" answered Fritz, so excited to have a traveling partner (and a talking fox at that) that he forgot the danger that awaited them.

"But can you just leave?" said the boy, looking around at the wealth of the fox's den.

The comforts of home were evident wherever he turned. A rich mahogany table with fanciful curved legs stood in the corner, and a pile of well worn leather books rested there in a stack. Pictures along the wall in ornate frames spoke of heavy years spent in this den, of roots put down that could not easily be pulled up. On one wall a tall grandfather clock, its great pendulum swinging methodically, kept a steady sweeping rhythm that swept away the seconds of their lives.

"Can I leave?" repeated Florian, leaping to his feet from out of the chair. "Of course I can leave! I should have left a long time ago! This den become a prison. I cannot roam and run and be happy here because of the Shadows. And all the contentment in the world is lost with no one to share in it. You see, I have not the one desire of my heart: a vixen with which to share the joys of life. All these beautiful things come to nothing when loneliness is thrown like a lock on my heart."

"Then you must come!" said Fritz, caught up in the mounting excitement of the fox's speech, leaping now to his own feet and almost spilling the coffee in his hand. "We will go over the mountains. Into the beyond and farther than that. We will find your vixen. We will find you Love. And we might also find that...well...that..."

"Yes, we might," said the fox and added, "Then, let us be off as quickly as possible."

"Yes, let's! Have you anything you want to take?"

The fox shook his head and said, "Nothing for me, except perhaps food for the road. We may take whatever stores from my pantry, for I think it will be long before ever I return here."

With that, the little animal led the way in a quick orange blur. It was obvious that the appearance of the boy had reawakened something in Florian that had slumbered for a long time; now awake, it demanded action.

The gathering of foodstuffs and provisions was accomplished in a flurry of movement, as the fox leapt here and there, tossing things to Fritz, who did his best to catch them all and stuff them into his knapsack. No sooner had he put two loaves of bread in the bag than a great block of sharp cheese flew at him, and then a couple of apples soared through the pantry, a few ears of corn, some tomatoes, and finally a tightly wrapped hunk of dried, salted meat.

After much bobbling and fumbling by the little boy, all the food was stored in his knapsack and though the bag was heavy, he said to the fox with a shrug, "It's not very much, is it?"

"It will be enough," said Florian with a confident smile, "And besides, we want to travel light. Travel fast."

As the two unlikely companions finished the last of their preparations for departure, Fritz shared with Florian the series of events that had led to his arrival on the fox's doorstep. As he told the animal of his encounter with the Watcher in the Wind, Florian listened intently and afterward, said:

"I myself have never spoken with the Watcher. But I have heard it said that he is very wise and very old, yet very Mysterious."

To each of these descriptions, the young boy agreed wholeheartedly. The Watcher had been a strange being, and yet all around had seemed to exude unfathomably deep wisdom.

When the boy told the fox what had been said of forks and keeping to the right, Florian nodded solemnly, as in the presence of great knowledge and insight, and said, "Yes, yes. Let us in all things keep to the right, my boy."

Fritz smiled and patted the fox on the shoulder and said, "Of course!"

For the little boy had still not learned the difficulty or the profound Mystery in such a statement.

And yet the fox, a creature of far superior age and experience, smiled in return for the boy's earnest pledge and his abiding innocence, even as they stood before the door, knowing the deadly Shadows waited outside.

Fritz put his hand on the golden doorknob and shivered, not from the cold of the metal, but from the sudden awareness that Death abode in the Lands Beyond the Moon, as surely as It stalked the shadows of the fields he'd known. The unseen, unknown Shadows filled his heart with a fear that he had not known yet, not even when he was fleeing from the wolves. His journey into these strange lands, so newly begun, had suddenly lost its air of fancy and lightness.

In its place was the knowledge that he could not turn back, no easier than he could stop the yearning in his soul, and yet he knew that to go on, to press forward, meant mortal danger. In the first steps up the mountain path, Fritz had considered nothing of the evil that may lie upon that road, but now, confronted with its unmistakable presence, the boy began to wonder if he had not, after all, taken on too big of a task for himself.

But even as these thoughts flashed through his mind, he pushed them away with all the bravado of a nine-year-old boy. And in the next second came a resurgent flood of the aching in his boyish heart. Fritz turned the golden doorknob, flung open the door, and said to the fox:

"Onward!"

Florian bounded into the cave entrance at Fritz's side, and with a sharp right turn, the pair hurried up the mountain path toward the fabled pass.

After that one word in the doorway, the two companions spoke nothing to each other for a long time and indeed, tried to make as little noise as possible. Although Fritz and Florian were filled with bravery in their every bone, they were not stupid. Unnecessary laughter or bold talk would only bring the Shadows upon them.

Even with the braveness that buoyed their attitudes, the two could not help casting sideways glances into dark cave mouths, or from stepping lightly past dim, moonlit crevices in the rocky land. The two mentioned nothing of this to each other, but both walked resolutely onward and upward.

When they came to a fork in the path, Florian immediately led the way up the right side of it, and Fritz followed. But as he did, the boy's eyes lingered even longer than before on the left side, noticing that it was level and smooth and as well-manicured as Mother's yard and looked like very easy walking. The right side that they had taken was strewn everywhere with sharp rocks that were unavoidable and that poked through the soles of Fritz's leather shoes.

Soon, the boy's feet became quite sore and if he'd had the nerve to speak of it (if the Shadows had not weighed so heavily on his mind), he would have complained about this very loudly to Florian. Also, the smell on this side of the road carried the foul odor of rotten eggs. As the pair walked, this odor grew stronger and stronger until Fritz put his hand over his nose and mouth and breathed shallowly.

When they came to a flat place like a landing, which seemed well protected from a sudden sneak attack by any creatures of the darkness, Fritz and Florian whispered to each other.

"What is that smell?" said the boy.

"Whatever it is, it is unpleasant," said the fox.

The boy thought this a bit of an understatement and mentioned to his companion, "I bet it did not smell like this on the left side of that last fork."

The fox frowned and shook his head at the comment. But a little while later, as the two continued walking and the smell became ever stronger and fouler, Florian himself thought back to that last fork and its smooth left side.

At one point on the march, Fritz had to pause and rub his sore feet with an exasperated moan. Yet for the most part, the pair went on noiselessly, up and up that unpleasant way. And soon enough, they came to another fork in the path, where it split away to the left and right around a massive boulder in the center.

Florian and Fritz looked keenly at the boulder, because this was no ordinary mountain stone. For one thing, its huge mass glimmered all over as if coated in metal of some sort, but this must have been some trick of their tired eyes. Tired eyes can see many bizarre sights under the dancing rays of the moon and stars, and they have done so often, even on the earthbound side of the Milky Way; how much more so in the Lands Beyond the Moon!

Yet this was not the only odd thing about this particular boulder. Fritz recognized at once those runes that he had seen before, the same unknown carvings that had been on the archway at the path's start and on the standing stone in the midst of the wild wood. The young boy walked up to the boulder and placed his hand on the etchings. They felt like ordinary scratches in stone and he rubbed his palm over them, feeling their edges slide under his skin.

Oh, how he wished he could read them!

After this, he turned to Florian the fox and said, "This is an important fork! No others have had such a marker."

Florian wrinkled his nose and cocked his head to one side, considering this. He said, "Maybe that is so. But what difference does that make? We should keep to the right, as you said. As the Watcher said."

Fritz nodded, rubbed his chin thoughtfully, and then turned and looked up either side of the fork.

"Maybe," he said to himself.

And he said this because now he was presented with an interesting choice. At this fork, the path on the left was undoubtedly the better looking.

Up the right side, the sharp rocks blanketed the whole of the road to the point that it looked unwalkable, and Fritz worried that the jagged stones would bloody his feet in a matter of seconds. There was also the matter of the smell, which wafted down from that way like a rancid wind of sour milk and rotten eggs and dead animals and several other worse smells that were so terrible in their putrescence that words cannot convey them. And worse than the smell was the unsettling darkness that swallowed all but the first few feet of the right side. The travelers could not see where it led, and this conjured up vague ideas in their minds.

The boy contrasted all of this with the left side of the fork. On that side—the side that up until now he had never even considered because of the Watcher's advice — was a smooth, well-kept road that was lined with a neatly tended fence, so pleasant that it could have been mistaken for some cottage dweller's front walk. It seemed a well-traveled road, too, as the outlines of many feet could be seen in the dust of it. The smell up that way was altogether different as well. Nothing could describe it but to say this: imagine the best smell in the whole universe (maybe it is your own mother's cooking or maybe it is the sweet and heavy scent of rain or maybe it is the perfume of a darling love); whatever it is, imagine that, and there you have the scent coming down from the left side of the fork!

In the end, that broad left side was altogether irresistible, all the more so because the bright rays of the moon behind them fell heavily on that side. The moonbeams lit the left side so that Fritz could see far, far up and could tell that the path wound on and on in relative ease for as far as his little eyes could make out.

Why not take the left side?

"Yes, why not take the left side?" asked Fritz, giving voice to that thought.

Florian stepped up to the boy and said, "What did you say?"

"I said, the left," answered the boy, pointing that way, "I mean, just look at it. How could anyone pick that way," and here he jabbed a scornful thumb back the right way, "How could anyone choose that when the left is so obviously the easier?"

"Are you sure?" said Florian, looking nervously back and forth, his acute foxy nose undoubtedly catching the difference in smell.

"Why, of course I am sure!" said the boy, his confidence in the left side growing by the second.

"But what about the Watcher's words?" said the fox, now wrinkling his nose with thoughtful uncertainty, "Ought we not to listen to the Watcher?"

Fritz's confidence flagged at the memory of those words, "keep to the right!" He felt ashamed for a fleeting moment, and yet...and yet...

"But just look for yourself!" he exclaimed to Florian, as he pointed to the left. "See how easy, how simple a walk it would be? I mean, shouldn't we trust our own eyes, our own judgment, here? How do we know that the Watcher is correct? How do we know anything at all, unless we find out for ourselves?"

"No, Fritz," said the fox, pleading with him, "We mustn't go that way. No matter how easy it looks! We must heed the Watcher. We must stay to the right."

But Fritz cast one last doubtful look at the difficult right side and capped off his speech with this:

"After all, who is to say the right is the right? Doesn't it all matter where you are standing? Isn't it all relative?"

And the boy had convinced himself. Indeed, many older and better educated men have asked these same questions and have sounded very intelligent while doing so and have doubtlessly come to the same wrong conclusion.

You see, the Truth is the Truth, and the right is the right and will always be the right, no matter how many fancy words are thrown at it or how ugly or difficult it may seem. The Watcher had known this, Florian had known it, and the boy Fritz had known it as well.

"Keep to the right!" were the words.

But Fritz went left.

Chapter 5

As these things tend to do, the journey up the left side went very well in the beginning. The well-trodden path rolled easily on, rising gently toward the craggy heights, and the two travelers hastened over it in the light of shimmering moonbeams. The sudden change in scent entranced them and made them feel much more relaxed and at ease in the mountains.

Earlier, the great worry of the Shadows weighed heavy on their minds, but now that seemed like such a distance problem. Even the bruises on Fritz's feet seemed less tender and felt like they healed by the second.

What a path this left side was!

Gone were the jagged rocks underfoot and gone was the horrid smell. In their place was a broad way that beckoned the travelers on with pleasant fragrance toward their destination. At this speed, Fritz felt sure that he and Florian would make the mountain pass in no time. The little boy could not wait to reach the other side of the summits.

Yet even as he thought these things, the path twisted sharply to the left and downward, descending away from the peaks. Fritz thought that maybe it just went down for a little while and then would rise again after the momentary dip. But the path continued sloping down and in fact, the decline became so steep that Fritz had to lean backward as he walked. He felt his leather shoes slip once or twice on the steepness.

"This is odd," said the boy to the fox, "Do you think it will go back up toward the West soon?"

"Surely it will," said the fox, "These mountain paths often meander and take a long time to get anywhere. At least the smell is not wretched."

Indeed, the gentle, enticing fragrance continued drawing them onward like a flower's bloom draws a bee. Yet Fritz was beginning to have serious doubts, and his mind kept going back to the fork, because no matter how hard he tried, he could not silence the Watcher's words that kept repeating in his head:

"Keep to the right!"

When the path dipped even more violently into a shadowed hollow in the rock, Fritz looked back up the way they had come. He said meekly:

"Maybe we ought to go back."

Florian the fox eyed the dark hollow suspiciously and said, "Yes, I think we made a terrible mistake ignoring the Watcher's advice."

"No, not so terrible," answered another voice, from somewhere in the darkness, "Not so terrible that you come this way."

The two traveling companions froze and their wide, frightened eyes met each other's. After a quiet second, Fritz called out:

"Who's there?"

The voice simply said, "It's not so terrible. Please, come on. Keep walking. Please."

There was a sudden sound of clicking, rapid clicking like a cane being tapped on a stone floor, or like the feet of some large insect skittering over the rock. A long, low sighing floated up from the dark hollow, like the sound of air being slowly let out of a blacksmith's bellows.

Fritz and Florian took a step back, and the boy asked again, "Hallo. Who is that?"

"Only me," said the voice, "But the others are near."

"The others? What others?"

"The other Lords of the Mountains."

"Oh, no!" cried Florian suddenly, his face contorted with fear, "That is the name the Shadows call themselves. It's one of them!"

Terror washed over Fritz like a plunge through the thin ice of a lake. He sank into the fear of a thousand stabbing knives, and he stood paralyzed beside his companion. Florian, for his part, crouched low into a fighting stance, all the red-orange hairs on his back standing straight up.

From down in the hollow came the dreadful hissing or sighing sound again, and vaguely through the gloom, the two wanderers saw a huge black mass lift itself up. The dreaded Shadow, scourge of the Mountains of the Moon, was stirring.

Florian growled and through the growls said, "I will fight by your side. But I do not think we can win. Even against one alone."

Fritz shuddered because he knew more Shadows were nearby.

"Then we have to run," said the young boy with sudden conviction. If they ever wanted to see more of the Lands Beyond the Moon, it was their only choice.

"Now!"

He and Florian turned and scrambled hastily back up the mountain path, sending pebbles and dust flying behind them. Up and up they ran, and behind came the sound of pursuing terror from the shadowed depths of the mountain.

Fritz dared not look back to catch a full glimpse of the beast. In the darkness of the hollow, he had seen only the indistinct outline of it and that had been more than enough to horrify his soul. He had no desire to see the Shadow in the full light of the moon, bearing down on him.

He and Florian focused all their energy on fleeing back to the fork as quickly as possible. This was not easy. Where before this left side had been so broad and easily traveled, it had now turned into an arduous journey and became, in some places, treacherously narrow. It passed over slender lips of rock that hung out above sheer drops, emptiness for thousands of feet below, and the companions were forced to cross these in single file.

Neither Fritz nor Florian could remember passing this way before, and neither could understand how the great, horrific Shadow managed to follow them over these precipices so quickly. Indeed, it seemed that no matter how fast the pair ran, the beast was just behind them, its weird claws clicking out a horrifying cadence on the stones. Its raspy breath was always just over their shoulders, and often Fritz felt that his end was only seconds away. The Shadow would eat both the young boy's and the fox's hearts.

When it seemed that the fear could not increase any more, suddenly there appeared other Shadows, leaping over boulders above them, scurrying over the face of the mountain like ants on discarded food. The whole rocky mountainside writhed and wriggled with the bodies of those terrible beasts.

The treacherous left path seemed to go on and on, and Fritz began to worry that they would never reach the fork. And so what if they did? The Shadows would surely pursue them past it.

Eventually he and Florian would be caught and eaten.

"Oh, why did I not listen? Why did I not keep to the right? I am so sorry!" said the boy.

With these words, Fritz ran as hard as he had ever run before. And suddenly, when all hope seemed lost, and when evil was nearest, there loomed before them the great, carved boulder.

It was the marker in the road. They had reached the fork!

And at that moment, something quite unexpected happened.

The huge stone, covered with those strange runes, began to glow with the radiance of a piercing blue Light. It shone so brightly that Fritz had to turn his eyes away. Into this welcoming glow ran the boy and his fox companion. In seconds, the deadly Shadows would fall upon them.

Or they would have, if not for the odd boulder and its Light.

For this shining blue began suddenly blasting off of the rock like sunrays taking flight. These blasts of white-blue Light shot through the deadly Shadows like arrows of fire through bundles of hay. And they produced much the same effect. The Shadows burst into flames, their grotesque bulging bodies suddenly consumed by this nameless power.

Fritz and Florian fell to their faces in fear and lay prostrate and trembling as the extraordinary brilliance flashed and flared and utterly destroyed the beasts that had pursued them. The uproar and pandemonium surrounded them with a deafening roar, and their hearts shrank inside of them in awe of such power. They dared not look up to see with their own eyes the terrible fate that befell the Shadows, for somehow they knew that such things were not to be seen by the eyes of the living.

When the confusion and disorder subsided, a heavy calm descended on that fork in the road, as gracefully as a dove alighting on a branch. In that moment, Fritz and Florian felt a resurgent peace within them, for they knew they had been saved by some power beyond their comprehension. The silence that filled that place afterward was so profound that Fritz, young though he was, knew he was in the presence of Holiness. For a long time, neither he nor the fox raised their eyes, but kept their foreheads pressed to the ground.

Then, sound returned in the form of a wispy wind that swept in with a swish and swirl and broke the spell. Fritz and Florian looked up and saw the boulder the same as they had seen it the first time; it was nothing but a large, strangely carved rock. Gone was the blue radiance, and gone was the feeling of power. Fritz looked around him at the mountains, but there was nothing to be seen. Only Florian's face told him that the experience had been real; where there had been fatigue before, there was now the fresh and smiling face of a fox.

Fritz realized that he, too, was smiling. He knew not why. He said nothing, because he knew that words meant nothing here. There were no words for such things.

Instead the young boy motioned to the right, and he and Florian took the way they should have taken before. The sharp rocks were still strewn all over the right side of the path, but Fritz bore the pain with a solid resolve. In fact, he was happy for the pain, for he knew the pass could not be far off.

And he was on the right road.

Chapter 6

The footfalls of the young boy and the trotting paws of the fox fell gently on the jagged road as they wound their way up to the pass. The soaring peaks of the Mountains of the Moon now looked close enough to touch. The pass through to the other side could not be far off.

Although the companions were out of danger, still they spoke nothing. All their focus was on reaching the pass and getting through it. What came after that, they knew not.

The air had turned bitterly cold as they walked higher, and little drifts of snow piled up in the crevices of the rock, blown there by the whispering wind. Now the path leveled out and became smooth, much to the relief of Fritz's sore soles. He and Florian could see ahead for a long straight stretch that ran to the north before turning sharply around a jutting corner of rock.

So straight was the road and so wall-like was that mass of rock that the two companions were sure that it had been crafted by someone or some Thing.

The mountain pass was finally at hand!

As the two hurried toward that turn ahead, still not speaking a word to each other, voices suddenly met their ears nonetheless. Fritz could not pick out any words, but it was as if a great multitude of speakers had begun talking at once. The voices flooded over the two companions like rushing water, and except for the surprise caused by their sudden occurrence, Fritz and Florian felt no fear at them.

The incoherent chorus sounded feminine, as of a great congregation of gentle women mumbling jumbled words all at once. Each spoke no louder than a murmur but together combined to make quite a noise upon the mountain air.

Fritz and Florian looked at each other in confusion, but as the voices did not seem threatening, the boy only shrugged his shoulders.

Louder and louder the womanly voices spoke, but still not a single intelligible word could be picked out of the mass of sound. The noise reached a crescendo as Fritz and Florian came to the corner.

As soon as the two turned toward the West, all became silent at once.

In front of the two travelers stretched the arrow-straight pass through the mountains, a narrow road paved with ancient cobblestones that cut through the peaks and far in the distance, descended into the beyond. Above them was the immense blackness of sky, that holy dark, the star-speckled canvas unbroken now, not even by the jagged peaks.

A hushed stillness lived in the pass. Watching over the place were massive stone sentinels in the shape of sphinxes, half-woman, half-lion creatures that Fritz had never before seen. These statues lined either side of the road, facing inward, their brooding gaze straight and unchanging.

"The Way of Silence," whispered Florian in awe.

And though Florian whispered these words, so quiet was the place that the fox's voice echoed and reverberated down the length of the pass. When the echoes died away finally, Fritz dared not reply. Somehow the boy knew that the silence here was meant to be unbroken.

He wondered at the place, and he wondered about the feminine voices that had come and gone so abruptly, and he wondered about a good deal many more things to which he gave no voice.

Without a word, Fritz put his hand on Florian's shoulder and together, they began their walk down the Way of Silence, beneath the eternal eyes of the expressionless sphinxes.

The two moved slowly, but their soft steps resounded in the silent pass. Fritz had the sudden thought that the sound might awaken those huge sculptures that lay peering into each other's dead eyes. Yet he and Florian walked on, past statue after statue, and not one of the stone visages stirred or took any notice of the small creatures creeping below them.

It took the travelers almost half an hour to walk the length of the Way of Silence, for the pass turned out to be longer than it had first seemed. All the while, the friends said nothing, but as they went on, their spirits rose. All the unpleasant fears that had followed them along the winding path up here disappeared.

When they passed by the last of the pairs of immense sphinxes, Fritz turned and looked back down the road. Away eastward, he could see the harvest moon still floating in the sky, and he knew that somewhere there, down the mountains and across the Milky Way, were his parents and his home.

Thought of home made him realize how far he had wandered, and a sudden pang of homesickness intruded upon his wanderings. His love of Mother and Father tugged at him. Yet this Love, strong though it was, was as drops in the ocean of his heart, and the greater part of him yet longed for the horizon, so that he knew he had much more wandering ahead of him. Even now, after treading the Way of Silence under the star-dotted expanse of the vast sky, the boy's yearning soul pushed him onward.

Frits turned his gaze away from home once more and looked forward into the West, where the slopes of the Mountains of the Moon descended into the Lands Beyond.

"We've made it through," he said, and he heard the words shake the silence behind them.

Florian gave a short bark, and the two companions began their descent. Their mood was positively delighted now. The brief brush with the Shadows was almost completely forgotten, and the only thing on their mind was the promise of the path in front of them.

They knew not where it would lead — Florian himself had never even been as far as the Way of Silence before and certainly not beyond — but they knew that they must follow it. The descent was much easier than the ascent, as is usually the case.

The path sloped gently down, and its curves were long and wide. Never did the road lead them close to a dangerous precipice or deadly drop. It kept right to safe parts of the mountainside, and so led the two travelers rather easily down from the heights.

The companions hoped that their journey would go on like this until the base of the mountains, but they soon discovered that it was not to be so. Suddenly a massive roiling cloudbank rolled over the western side of the mountain range, like a churning white wave that crashed over them with soundless power. Visibility fell to nothing almost immediately, so that Fritz could not even see the bright orange fur of his companion only feet away from him.

The descending path stayed nice and easy, but with their sight so restricted, the journey took longer than it should have. All the while, they could not see any of the land toward which they traveled. From such an incredible height, the two should have been able to see miles and miles of the Lands Beyond the Moon. But all that was visible was the endless drifting sea of white.

As the pair dropped in elevation, and the soaring peaks receded behind them, the temperature warmed. Fritz's teeth stopped their rapid chattering, and the normal color came back to his nose, which had been bright red in the frigid air of summits. Lower and lower they went, and vegetation now began to appear on either side of them.

With the clouds still heavy around them, Fritz and Florian could not see much of the growth, but what they could make out told them they were undoubtedly in a special place. The fertile mountainsides brimmed with life, and the colors of the wildflowers were of such fantastical hues and scents that Fritz could not believe he was seeing them. Even within the dense clouds, the blooms popped with vivid fuchsia, cerulean, indigo, and canary yellow. Fritz's astonishment at these flowers took his words away. Yet even Florian the fox who had frolicked in many mountain meadows could not name these peculiar flowers.

So the pair traveled on, marveling at the variety and intensity of the flora.

"What beauty!" said the fox, "What splendor!"

But the boy Fritz said nothing, absorbing every detail of these remarkable slopes. How gorgeous it would have been on a clear summer's day!

Soon, sounds began to creep into the picture. These drifted in, faint at first but steadily growing louder, from somewhere in the fog; the twittering and chirping of songbirds in unseen trees, the faint barking of some distant and concealed canine ("Might be a cousin," said Florian) and above all this, the gushing of a swift mountain river. Once or twice, Fritz thought he heard a soft giggle or whispered word, and he wondered if these belonged to that same multitude of feminine voices that had risen up on the mountain heights. When he mentioned this to Florian, the fox said:

"Maybe. I imagine that will not be the last time we hear from them. And I should think that we will encounter things more strange and wonderful than that the farther we go into the Lands Beyond the Moon.

Fritz smiled in agreement and his heart leapt at the prospect.

The more Fritz heard the fleeting voices drifting in the fog, the more he thought of those old fireside tales that he had heard from his grandparents, stories of a peculiar magical folk that sometimes crept out of the woods to steal a child, or else to make general mischief. These had been the tales of his childhood, the tales that had thrilled his young heart and had first lit the fire in his soul and stoked it to an irresistible flame. As he remembered these legends, Fritz said:

"Do you think those could be the voices of fairies?"

Florian looked around at the swirling wall of mist and said, "Perhaps. I have often heard of the Fairy Folk traveling abroad, even as far as your lands. But they make their mischief around Midsummer, don't they? And here it is the damp, cold fall. What might bring out so many of them on such a night?"

"I don't know," said Fritz, shaking his head thoughtfully.

The fog certainly did make this an unpleasant night. Fritz had never seen a fairy before and a part of him wished to, perhaps just not this night. The stories of those strange folk snatching babies from their crib never to be seen again filled Fritz with uneasiness about encountering any fairies on these foggy heights. In truth, there were just as many stories of the faith and kind charity and the many marvels of the Fairy Folk, but it is hard for a young boy to remember good stories in the dense night fog of a strange land; the frightful tales are much more easily recalled.

The dancing voices faded eventually, and now only the occasional indecipherable word could be heard on the air. Their journey went on for more downward sloping miles, until the young boy began to tire. His feet ached and his legs felt heavier than ever. Thinking back over the many adventures of this one night, it was a wonder that he could even remain standing. Now the exhaustion crept in on him, and he wished to find some shelter to bed down for awhile.

His wish would soon be rewarded.

The landscape (or what they could see of it in the mist) turned from flowering mountainside to high rolling hills, thickly grown over with high, even grasses, like well-groomed pastures in the sky. The travelers could see only a few yards of these hills in the fog, but their general outline stretched away into the shapeless distance. The path twisted through this wavy landscape, the faint traces of moonlight gleaming over the supple, swishing blades of grass.

A bleating came to them on the wind then, as of hundreds of sheep scattered through the hills, calling to each other in the formless fog. *Baa, baa*, sang the night choir, a lonesome melody in the shifting haze. Not a sheep did Fritz and Florian see, but the bleating echoed and answered from every direction. The green hills must have been full of sheep grazing on the rich grass.

The two travelers went on, and the mountain river they had heard earlier now sounded close at hand. Indeed, as they came down a small slope, a rushing gush of water ran just to the right of the road. Happily, the pair followed alongside, moving faster now for the road had straightened out along the direct line of the river.

Here they saw finally one of those sheep that was bleating so. The animal had its head down, drinking from the edge of the cool running water, and it looked up suddenly at the approach of the two strangers. It stood calmly watching them for a few moments as Fritz and Florian drew close. Then, it started from the bank and darted downstream, clearly frightened by the appearance of a sharp-toothed fox.

"I wouldn't have hunted it," said Florian, "I am not that cruel. That creature clearly belongs to someone's flock. It needn't be afraid."

"I know," said Fritz, "Let's follow it. It seemed to run in our direction anyway."

So they did.

And soon enough, they found the place to which the animal had run. On the riverbank stood a handsome little cottage, half-timbered and with a water wheel jutting out into the

Rushing River, turning now with the rapid strength of the flow. A neat little fence ran around the place and reminded Fritz of his own home so far away behind the mountains.

The cottage was set just inside a small grove of trees and their branches spread shade over the house and its little outbuildings: a small shed, a stable and a pen for sheep. In this pen were a number of sleeping ewes and kids, but it was evident that most of the flock was turned out this night. This accounted for the widespread bleating on the hilltops.

"I am tired," said Fritz, "Do you think we should ask to stay the rest of the night here?"

"I cannot imagine anyone of evil heart would ever live in a place so peaceful," said Florian, staring pensively at the charming cottage, "Why don't we have a look?"

The fox and the boy trotted up the front walk and rapped lightly on the oak door. There was no answer. Fritz knocked again, louder this time, ready with a sincere apology to the awakened owner should he come to the door with a frown at being disturbed at this hour.

Yet again there was no answer.

Fritz looked at Florian and then back at the dreary road. He said, "I cannot go any farther this night. I will collapse from sleepiness."

Florian nodded and said, "Maybe we ought to just try the door."

Fritz followed this advice and found the door unlocked. The heavy oak swung easily open.

"Hallo!" called out Fritz into the dim rooms beyond the threshold.

There was no answer.

"There must be no one home," said Florian, padding lightly into the foyer and sniffing at the air.

The inside of the house was as handsomely decorated as the outside, and even in the darkness, the travelers could see richly furnished rooms and grand tapestries hanging on the wall. It must have been quite a rich shepherd who dwelt here.

Fritz said, "I do not think we should just barge in like this."

Yet he kept walking deeper into the house.

"You're right, of course," said Florian, leading the way up the stairs, "It is rather rude. But certainly the owner would not begrudge the use of his house for one night. Why, we may even be gone before he arrives home and then he will never know the difference!"

The boy still felt bad about sneaking into a house that was not his, but Florian had a good point and besides, he was awfully tired. Fritz could not bear to think of going back out on the fog-covered road tonight. When he saw the bedrooms, he was convinced.

In a bedroom that looked out over the river waited a massive bed, taller even than he was. He needed Florian's help to scramble up the side onto the plush mattress. The sheets were as soft as meadow grass and smelled as fragrant. Florian hopped nimbly onto the bed and took his place near the foot. He turned a couple of circles as canines like to do when they settle in for the night, and then he plopped down with a heavy sigh on the rich blankets. Fritz was asleep almost as soon as he rested his head on the pillow.

Neither one knew what they would wake up to.

Chapter 7

When Fritz stirred from sleep, he somewhat expected to awake in his own bed with the sounds of Mother and Father preparing breakfast in the kitchen below, the whole adventurous night having been nothing but a fanciful dream brought on by his midnight snacking.

Yet it was no dream.

He still lay in the great comfortable bed in the unknown shepherd's cottage, Florian the fox curled cozily near his feet, and shimmering sunrays falling through the window to play on the furniture like fawns frisking and romping through a field. Fritz sat up and breathed in fully the fresh air. He had never slept so soundly, so deeply, so restfully in his entire life. Every inch of him felt restored.

Why, he felt like he could climb over another mountain range if he had to!

When the young boy excitedly swung his legs over the edge of the bed, the fox lifted his narrow head and said:

"What a sleep!"

Then he stood on all fours and gave himself a good shake that started with a little wiggle at the end of his shiny, black nose and spread like ripple through water down his back, to end finally in a great wag of his tail. He smiled at the boy and said:

"I feel positively full of life!"

Here, the fox jumped back and forth on the soft blankets, his head bowed low and his tail high in the air, wagging vigorously. A playful growl started in his throat and he jumped at Fritz, who sat dangling his feet over the edge of the bed. The fox bawled over the young boy, who sprawled out on his back, wrestling and laughing with joy.

When the lighthearted romp was over, Fritz sighed and wondered what lay ahead of them on their journey. Florian, for his part, had his mind on much more immediate matters.

"I'm hungry," he said and leapt over the edge of the bed.

Fritz dropped his feet to the cool floor and realized his own hunger. He said, "I left my knapsack with our food downstairs at the front door."

He passed through the door with Florian following him. The fox said, "Maybe we oughtn't eat our own supplies just yet. We do not know how long we will need them to last. Maybe there is some food in the cottage we could eat."

Now, Fritz had to stop his companion.

"I don't think so. We've already taken a night of rest here without permission. You said yourself you are no thief. I don't think it is right to steal food."

Florian nodded, somewhat shamefaced, and said, "You are right, of course. I am sorry. We foxes from the Mountains of the Moon do have a bit of ancestral thievery in us, I'm afraid. You see, my ancestors once came from your lands, many centuries ago, and I think those foxes there are all thieves and bandits and savages still."

"Oh, yes," said Fritz, thinking back to how Father spoke of foxes and other such animals of the night, "They steal chickens and eat what isn't theirs all the time. And they certainly don't talk or think like you do."

"My family has tried to cultivate a sense of civilization since coming to the Lands Beyond the Moon," said Florian the fox, straightening up proudly, "Beginning, first and foremost, by learning to speak. But occasionally, to my great embarrassment, we will slip back into some trait of our less civilized ancestors. Forgive me."

"Do not worry," said Fritz, thinking of all the savage men he had heard of, men who ravaged and pillaged by the sword, "You are not the only species who slips into savagery. Still, it is not right to steal, and I will not do it here."

He led Florian to the front door where the knapsack rested in the same spot that he had wearily dropped it last night. The pair went into the kitchen where stood two chairs and a table with nothing on it but salt and pepper shakers in the center.

Fritz plopped the knapsack on the table and began to sort through its contents. From inside he pulled a loaf of bread, the block of sharp cheese and a couple of ears of corn. He placed these in the center of the table. He looked around the kitchen, found a drawer filled with silverware and rummaged in it until he found a knife.

"We will just borrow it," he said with a grin at Florian.

Then, the two companions broke bread, cut morsels off the tasty cheese and munched on the corn. When they finished with their small breakfast, Fritz leaned back in his chair and patted his belly.

Now that his hunger was satisfied, the boy was anxious to get back on the road. When he said as much to Florian, the fox said:

"I had hoped to meet the owner of this fine cottage. But you are right. We should be off while the day is young."

So Fritz rinsed the knife off with a pail of water near the sink, returned it to its place in the drawer, and hefted his knapsack onto his shoulder. Then, he and Florian went out the front door.

What a sight awaited them as they stepped out of the cottage!

Autumn's morning sun shone brightly and warmly, throwing its brilliant rays over everything in sight. The heavy fog of last night was but a distant memory, and the land that it had obscured now burst upon them in all its magnificence and splendor. To describe this hilly landscape at all is to do it injustice, for no words could match the glory of the vista that met Fritz's and Florian's eyes that morning.

For miles around rolled those green hills, so abundant and fertile that life, in all its splendid variety, blossomed and sprouted from every single inch of land. Some of the more distant hilltops showed a smattering of white dots, and it took Fritz a while to figure out that these were sheep grazing far away. Nearer at hand, there were dancing fields of emerald grasses, so thick and lustrous that the blades reflected the sunrays in a thousand gleaming beams.

Fritz had never seen such a land, still flourishing even as the days of autumn came on hard. Back home, the trees of the wild wood would have been shivering with the year's cold death, and winter's snows would not be far off.

Here, however, only the changing leaf colors of the trees showed any sign that fall had reached this place. Yet somehow even these reds and oranges and yellows seemed frightfully alive, throwing off such vibrancy that Fritz almost had to shade his eyes. Such beauty only threw fuel on the fire of his soul; the distant horizon, so wonderful and remote, pulled at him all the more powerfully.

The sound of the merrily running river serenaded this landscape, its water gushing and rushing with all its strength down from the Mountains of the Moon, spinning the waterwheel of the cottage with melodic splashes.

Fritz breathed in the smell of unnamed flowers; the sweet intoxication of nature's own perfume filled his nostrils and spread throughout his energetic body. He could have run headlong into one of the gently sloping pastures, tramping through the high grass, if he had not heard another sound then.

The bleating of hundreds of sheep came to them from just around a bend up the road eastward. This was the same direction from which the two had journeyed last night. Now from that way, it sounded as if the whole flock of sheep that they had heard last night spread over the foggy hills was gathered together on the road. *Baa, baa*, bleated the marching army, and here they swept around the curve.

On they marched, a huge mass of white wooly backs coming calmly toward them, and in the front, leading the way, walked a young shepherdess with a staff resting across her shoulders. If the beauty of that landscape could have been made into a person, she would have failed to match the beauty of this young maiden.

She smiled and the radiance of her joyfulness drove shadows into hiding. Her hair shone golden blonde in a tight halo braid around her head. This angelic maiden strode barefoot over the land, her staff balanced on her shoulders, one arm slung over the stick and her hand dangling carelessly as she stepped lightly down the road. No doubt she was the owner of the cottage, though such a beautiful girl seemed to belong in nothing less than the most lavish palace.

Her clothes were those of a simple shepherdess, but something in her eyes spoke of riches unfathomable, of a renowned ancestry covered by poor clothes, as cloud covers a sun but cannot dim its glory. It was clear that though she played the part well and naturally, this girl was no simple peasant. Her long skirt flowed as gracefully as a princess as she swept down the hill before her sheep.

When her shining eyes caught sight of the boy and the fox, she stopped in the road, and her flock halted behind her. She was only a stone's throw from them, and she stood staring at the two travelers with a look of innocent surprise and then with delight, until Fritz thought that he would fall to his knees in front of her, so dazzled was the young boy by her loveliness. When she spoke, it was the sound a pure heart would make if it could be turned into a musical instrument.

"Hallo! And good morning to you, travelers!"

Fritz blushed, as if he had just been kissed; for such was the warmth of her greeting that it felt like a loving embrace. Florian wagged his tail and let out a cheerful bark. When Fritz managed to gather his wits, he bowed graciously and said:

"Hallo and good morning, shepherdess. Might you be the one who lives in yonder cottage?"

"I am she," said the graceful maiden, lowering her staff and leaning her lithe form serenely on it.

"Hanna is my name. And who might you be, young one?"

"I am Fritz," said the boy, bowing slightly again, "And my companion, the fox Florian from the Mountains of the Moon."

"At your service," said Florian and bowed his muzzle low to the ground in reverence of the lovely shepherdess.

"We are traveling into the Lands Beyond," said Fritz, pointing away to the West, "And we have just come down from the mountains."

"Through the Way of Silence?" said Hanna breathlessly, although something in the way she said it told the travelers she already knew the answer. She eyed them now with a look of knowing admiration mixed with brimming delight and said, "Not many come through that pass. What draws a child from the forests and the distant fields he knows to these Lands Beyond the Moon?"

When Fritz did not answer for many long seconds, the shepherdess grinned a playful grin and said:

"You needn't answer if the answer is what I know it to be. The secrets of your heart are yours alone, to keep and to carry. Merrily will I help you and gladly will I speed you on! But come, let us not tarry in the middle of the road."

Then, she touched Fritz lightly on the shoulder and led him back to the cottage with the great host of sheep following and Florian trotting alongside. With a swift wave from the shepherdess' staff, the sheep trotted obediently into the great pen, and soon it filled with so many white bodies that it looked like the maiden had trapped a roving cloud in that pen.

Without a word, she led the travelers to the front door of the cottage. There, she stopped and said, "I am so very glad that you two stayed the night here. Beautiful though this land is, it can be dangerous at night, especially in such a fog. And there is no place more welcoming for a weary traveler than a warm bed."

Fritz's jaw hung open in astonishment, and then in embarrassment.

"But how did you…"

Hanna waved her hand in dismissal of the question and said, "Oh, but you mustn't think that I am upset, or that you were not welcome. Why, of course you were welcome! And I am only upset that I could not be here to host you. I spent the night in the open air, tending the flocks."

Now, she threw open the door and said:

"Come back inside. Rest a while and let us speak of things to come. Then, you may be off."

She placed her staff near the door and glided through the rooms beyond like a feather on the wind. And now the house appeared utterly transformed from the place that Fritz and Florian had seen last night. The shepherdess seemed to fill every room with Light, as if a hundred shutters had just been thrown open. Her brilliant warmth gave life to the cottage that made last night's view of it dim and drab in comparison.

She passed into the kitchen, and the two travelers followed her. By the time they reached the room, a sumptuous spread was laid on the table, a breakfast fit for royalty; there were steaming plates of bacon, smoked salmon that must have been caught from the river, and several loaves of freshly baked bread of different varieties, all smelling so delicious that Fritz's mouth immediately began watering.

For a sweet end to their meal, the young boy saw heaped plates of pies, strudels and sugary cakes of all kinds and all colors, more than he had ever seen in his life. The two travelers stood in wonder at how a meal could have been produced so quickly.

"Do not look so surprised!" said Hanna, giggling as she spoke, "You are in the Lands Beyond the Moon. How then should this be odd?"

Fritz and Florian smiled and took their seats at the table. Though they had already eaten, it had been a rather meager meal of stale food from a traveler's knapsack. They knew that they would tread many miles this day, and they wanted all the strength they could get.

Hanna the shepherdess whispered a few words of a language that Fritz did not understand, but he recognized them as words of blessing. And when this was done, they all three began eating. The food tasted like the first glimmer of sun after a long storm.

The young boy's hunger was deeply satisfied, and never had been it satisfied more delightfully and deliciously. As they ate, the blonde maiden studied both the boy and the fox. She herself ate but little, and between dainty bites, she spoke to them.

"What you seek in the Lands Beyond the Moon, you will find. But you may not find it in the way you expect. There are many paths to take. You must let your restless heart lead. For just as there is great Good, so there is untold evil in these lands."

The talk of paths brought to Fritz's mind the advice of the Watcher, and he shared this now with the maiden.

Hanna smiled and said:

"The Watcher in the Wind is a great Comforter, and you are lucky to know Him. Heed His words. But I say to you now, there will come times when the Watcher's words alone cannot help you. In those terrible moments, you must lean not on comfort, but on action. You must heed the Word that is pure Act."

Her words were frightening and strange to the boy, but tempered so by her beauty and by the flow of her tender voice.

She put out both her hands and placed one on top of Fritz's and one on Florian's paw, and said:

"You go into a land beset by evil. Down from these hills, you will pass into a valley called the Vale of Abundance, but you will find only unrest there. Those lands are ruled from the Castle in the Sky. There has been much mischief and evildoing in those parts, and the rightful rulers have much trouble, yea, much and more."

The two travelers had finished eating and listened closely to the troubling sayings that Hanna spoke. They felt glad for the strength the food gave them, because the next words from the shepherdess were more worrisome still:

"You must help them with these tribulations. You must drive out the evil from the Lands Beyond the Moon."

Chapter 8

"We?" said Fritz, astonished, "Florian and I? But we are so small! How can we do such a thing?"

"Here is a Mystery: the smallest will be made great," said Hanna with a compassionate bow of her head, "And the mighty brought low. You have come far, but you will go farther. You go to do things of great renown, though yet you know them not."

She turned to Florian and said, "And you, fox of the Mountains of the Moon, will be a loyal friend, steadfast, of true heart, and you will redeem that race of canines known for their trickery and guile. And they will sing of Florian the Faithful, and never again speak of deceit or of the fickleness of foxes in the Lands Beyond the Moon."

The two travelers sat speechless, wondering at these lofty sayings, and they knew not how to respond. Here was a maiden beyond comprehension and she was making pronouncements that pierced their hearts.

When she finished speaking, she stood and led them out of the cottage, their bodies brimming with strength and energy. The shepherdess took up her staff and standing in her doorway, pointed far away to the West, and said:

"Go, small ones, go and seek your soul's longing in the Lands Beyond the Moon. Do not tarry at the starting line, though the race be dangerous and difficult. Run on and finish your course! Go to the very ends of all, and see what may be seen. But do not be blind or ignorant. Know this: there will come upon you those who wish your destruction. Yet, even still, go with the peace that passes all understanding."

The two companions took to the road again, and waved to the beautiful blonde maiden, and Fritz's heart was sore to leave one so lovely. As they walked, he cast many looks over his shoulder, and each time he looked, he saw the shepherdess standing in her door, waving her delicate hand to them, her eyes shining and her smile never fading. The cottage of the shepherdess receded into the distance, little by little, until the road dipped down the side of a hill, and the lovely maiden fell out of sight.

Now, Fritz turned his eyes to the West, to where his feet led him, to where unknown dangers waited. He was glad for such a companion as Florian, and he did not for a second doubt Hanna's words about the fox's faithfulness. Florian trotted alongside him, looked up with a smile and said:

"I am happy you blundered past my den. Already I have lived more in the last day than in many years before it. Whatever the end, I am glad to have made you my friend."

Fritz patted him on the back and said, "I will always be your friend."

And the young boy meant it, as only children can speak such a phrase with unconditional sincerity.

So the two journeyed on, through the rolling hills west of the Mountains of the Moon, and the road wound on and on, up and down over the wavy land. Nothing of importance happened to them in this hill country. They saw a few scattered sheep on the hills, grazing contentedly under the warmth of the midmorning sun, but whether these belonged to Hanna's flock or to another's, the companions did not know. They spied a couple of cottages, far off in the distance, barely discernible on the horizon, only standing out against the backdrop of clear blue sky because of the gray haze of smoke that drifted from their chimneys.

None of these houses were near the road, however, and Fritz and Florian walked through what was mostly wilderness, fresh and untamed, untouched by the changeable cruelties of civilization. Now, trees grew more abundant as the hills rolled down and the soil and air became more welcoming to the towering elms and cottonwoods and massive oak trees festooned with hanging moss. Countless unseen birds chattered in harmony as they watched the odd pair pass beneath them.

Many miles passed under their feet, and the boy and fox made idle conversation to pass the time. The morning drew close to noontime and the day turned very un-autumnally warm. Yet it was as pleasant a day as has ever existed on either side of the moon, and Fritz and Florian enjoyed their trek.

They came to the ends of the hill country, where the last of the rolling feet of the mountains ceased and gave way to flat, green plains in a rich bottomland. Fritz and Florian paused on this last hill, beneath the shade of a swishing cottonwood, and beheld the vast spread of the valley below.

There was no doubt that this was the Vale of Abundance, of which Hanna had spoken. The whole valley flowered with life. There were thriving crops that could be seen in the distance, and large stretches of wooded land for lumber. The Rushing River provided a fresh steady supply of clear mountain water to the valley. Fritz could see far below in the shimmering distance, the sprawl of a good-sized city that lay open beneath the sky and its broad encircling wall marked out the city's perimeters on the valley floor.

He guessed this city to be about ten miles away. Between that city's gates and the two travelers, at the bottom of the sloping hill, ran the Rushing River, the very same that flowed from the mountains past the shepherdess' cottage so far away now. Beyond the western bank of that river was a wide expanse of greensward, a great flat and open pasture. This even land ran unbroken for miles to the city's edge. The bright green grasses were neatly trimmed to a fine length, perhaps from grazing herds or flocks.

Yet no livestock filled that open space now. As Fritz and Florian watched, they saw two huge masses assembled on either side of that sprawling field, to the north and the south. It did not take the boy long to figure out that these masses were made of men and were, in fact, armies arrayed for war. From their vantage point on the hillside, the boy and the fox could make out brilliant banners flapping in the wind, displaying the heraldry of places and peoples unknown.

The armies were large, and the banners were many on each side, so that it seemed the whole host of the Lands Beyond the Moon was emptied upon the field. The battle lines had been drawn, and though Fritz could not guess what the conflict was, he knew that he was soon to witness a mighty clash on the open field.

For fleeting moments, Fritz was filled with equal parts excitement and terror. How many times has a young boy wished for battle, longed for the excitement of the flying banners and the pounding feet of heavy chargers and the breaking of shields and the swinging of swords? How many times have grown men wished for the same?

And yet here was the very promise of such a day, and Fritz found himself wishing only that he could put a stop to it. Men would lose their lives this day. Men would meet their bloody and irrevocable end down there on the field, and their passing would be forgotten as easily as the passing of the leaves every fall. Fritz listened with growing anticipation and dread as the trumpets of war sounded firmly in the distance.

The lines began to move, as surely and unstoppably as the seasons of the year, and Fritz and Florian could only watch as they drew inevitably closer.

"It will be a terrible battle," said Florian gravely, "Yet the numbers seem to favor those from the south."

"I feel we should do something," said Fritz, "But there is nothing to be done when men are intent on killing each other."

Fritz, young though he was, had already learned this fact.

So the two travelers watched as the charge was taken up, and the surging armies rushed forward into pitched battle. When the lines met, there roared the sickening crash of steel and bone at once, and the sound reached the two on the hillside, delayed but a second by the great distance. The shouts and screams of dying men mixed with the shouts and screams of triumphant warriors and created a storm of drifting echoes that resounded with the terror of war.

Through the air flew whistling flocks of barbed death as the arrows of a hundred archers sang out from twanging bowstrings. Where these arrows fell exactly, Fritz and Florian could not see, but as they struck, there came a new wave of screams from the men who had been hit.

For a long time, the vicious blood work went on in that green place, and although the numbers had favored the south, the army of the north side put up a determined resistance. Fritz stood in awe as he witnessed the skillful maneuvering of units. The men-at-arms marched or ran in formation, only to crash headlong into their opposing forces and take up the battle again.

Now great columns of cavalry men rode hard on both sides, moved around by skilled generals as easily as pieces on a chessboard. But who would win this day, whose strategy would prevail, or who would checkmate his opponent?

So the battle played out, with Fritz and Florian watching and saying little, until it became evident that the south side would overpower the north through sheer numbers. Wave after wave of infantry men, swordsmen and spearmen, rushed forward to their deaths, only to be replaced by more waves, until they had beaten back the northern army. Then came a last harrowing charge of the south's mounted lancers and heavy cavalry, charging with all speed into the lines of the other army and cutting through the enemy as spring's rivers thunder down from the mountains.

With a great cry of grief, the northern army sounded its retreat and its men fled for their very lives before the pursuit of their enemy. Fritz could watch no longer, for the battle was over and had been lost by one side and won by another, and yet still the killing would go on. That seemed wrong, for what was the necessity of killing your enemy if he has been so utterly beaten? It seemed a cruel and heartless thing to pursue the fleeing and broken army.

Fritz and Florian sat beneath the cottonwood tree for a long time, no longer caring to watch the field, but knowing that they must pass that way soon. Their destination had been the lands to the

West, and the near city looked as good a place as any to start.

"I wonder what the battle was about," said Fritz, finding it hard to put the thought of it from his mind, "I wonder why they were fighting."

"There are always reasons to fight if one looks for them," said Florian, lying on his stomach with his head on his paws. "Some reasons are better than others, and it is not always wrong to shed blood, though always unpleasant. Let us hope that at least one side today had right and just reasons for such a thing."

The sound of the distant armies now faded entirely, and nature's quiet returned to their little shaded spot. Fritz stood and knew that it was time.

"Let's go down," he said to the fox.

The path toward the greensward was easily traveled and it led straight to the Rushing River's edge. The path crossed the water at a handsome stone bridge. This little arch led the travelers out onto the first grasses of that green place, and already they could see, hear and smell the remnants of battle.

Some yards away lay discarded weapons on the greenery, cast aside by fleeing soldiers or lost and dropped by dead men. Fritz and Florian left the road to walk through the field, and they picked their way through these scattered swords and axes gingerly and with great reverence. Soon they came upon blades of grass stained with blood, and blades of steel stained with yet more, and their reverence grew. This field had been consecrated, set aside as hallowed ground this day, baptized by shed blood.

When they came upon the first of the dead men, Fritz fell to his knees and wept openly, and Florian's tears fell as well. Fritz had never seen a dead body in person before, and these men had met the most dramatic and visible of all ends. Some had been run through with swords and spears, others had been trampled violently by horses, and still others had had various limbs lopped off. The young boy saw enough carnage that day that forever afterward he would always look first for the peaceful solution to a problem, and only with great reluctance and after much searching, would he ever resort to just violence.

It is hard to be for war when you have seen its results firsthand.

"I never thought I would see death like this when I came to the Lands Beyond the Moon," said Fritz.

"I am afraid we will see much more before our journey is through," said Florian, remembering the words of the beautiful shepherdess Hanna.

"You are right," said Fritz, staring out over the great expanse of battlefield at the broken banners lying strewn around the broken bodies of men. Already crows and other carrion birds circled the battlefield. Fritz's heart ached to think of these bodies left to the birds of the air and the beasts of the earth, but there was nothing that he and Florian could do.

Their work was westward, and this was not their affair.

"We should go to the city away yonder," said the boy, pointing.

Florian agreed, and they made their way back over the wretched battlefield to the road. This they followed toward the gates of the city westward, both of them wondering what strange and frightening marvels awaited them inside.

Chapter 9

The walk to the city took about an hour, for the travelers kept a good pace. In truth, they wanted to put distance between themselves and that terrible battlefield. They thought they would feel much safer within the city walls that now showed themselves on the horizon.

These walls rose higher and higher before them, all made of white-washed stone, so that the whole city seemed built from the finest porcelain. This gave the tall, thin turrets a dainty look, although the armed men that manned the walls looked anything but dainty. The gates of the city were shut tight, probably for safety from the warfare taking place so nearby.

This was no warrior city. The closer the two travelers came to it, the more it showed itself to be a den of merchants, a cheaping-town as they were called in those days, a place where men bought and sold all sorts of goods. Just outside the city's gate were wagons that had been abandoned in the apparent haste to get within the city. These wagons were all overloaded with foods, wares, and merchandise, as if they had been carted from distant farms and distant lands to be sold at the bustling marketplace.

Yet not a soul could be seen in the market that stood fast to the gate of the city. It was one of those markets that pop up just beyond city gates so that they can service the constant flow of men and women in and out of the city, but all was abandoned now. The only things moving were Fritz and Florian and a few horses that idly nibbled grass and paid no mind to the affairs of men.

When the two travelers reached the massive gate, Fritz hesitantly knocked on a small porthole in a side door. When no guard answered, he knocked louder and louder. Still no answer came, and for a moment, it seemed that they would not get into the city this day.

"Yell for someone," said Florian.

Fritz nodded and said, "Hallo! Open up! We wish to come inside the city!"

A few seconds passed in silence, and then came the sound of running feet, and suddenly the small eyeslot in the gate was slid furiously open.

"Who wishes?!" yelled the gruff guard, his eyes scowling at them from the narrow slot. He was a man, a human that is (you never know what you may find in the Lands Beyond the Moon), and from the sound of his voice, quite a large and ill-tempered man.

"I say, who wishes to come in? Don't you know there is killing going on out there?"

"Yes, we do," said Florian as politely as he could.

"That is why we wish to come inside," added Fritz.

"Well, why didn't you get inside earlier?!" shouted the guard, "The curfew was final! You should have been inside then! Before the battle! Now be gone! Off our doorstep, before you join the dead and become food for the crows!"

The slot slammed shut, and the sound of tramping boots disappeared inside the city.

Fritz looked at his companion and said, "Well…what now?"

The fox shook his head and stared high up at the ramparts that towered above them.

"I don't suppose it is any use to try to climb over," he said.

Fritz opened his mouth to reply, but another voice interrupted him.

"Oh, no, you will never climb over," it said, "Can't be done. Simply cannot be done. No way. No how."

"Who said that?" said Fritz and Florian at the same time, looking all around.

The speaker turned out to be a rather small gentleman, dressed in green finery and neat little trousers, and sitting cross-legged on a small ox-cart behind them. His face was ruddy, flushed as if from too much heat, but he looked quite comfortable, sitting there with wiggling toes visible through his boots, as merry as a child who has just eaten a scrumptious dessert and been offered seconds by a generous host.

In one hand, he held a long stemmed pipe and puffed lightly at it, sending some clouds of rich smoke drifting above him. He was happily examining the two travelers as a man examines livestock that he is about to purchase and finds them adequate. The man hopped off the ox-cart and said:

"I said it, and I meant what I said. You will never climb over that wall. Believe me! I've tried." Here, he lowered his pipe, exhaled a great cloud of smoke, and bowed.

"My name is Reginald Dumont. At your service."

"I am Fritz," said the boy, "And this is my companion, Florian. And we are at yours."

"Why have you tried to climb this wall before?" said the fox, skipping the pleasantries and getting right to business, "That seems an odd thing to do. Why didn't you just go in before the curfew?"

"Ah ha," said Reginald, raising his smoldering pipe, "Why didn't you?"

"Well, we weren't here before the curfew, or the battle," said Fritz, "We've only just arrived."

"And I was not allowed in," said Reginald, gracefully waving his arm in front of him as if beckoning someone in through a door, "By the very same charming guard who just slammed the door in your face."

Now the boy and the fox eyed this exiled stranger warily. Fritz said, "Why were you not allowed in?"

"Excellent question, dear boy!" said the small gentleman, and wiggled his finger before him as he gave the following speech:

"I will tell you why! The men of this town are, quite simply, the most corrupt and irredeemable of all the dirty dealers in any of the inhabitable lands. Dishonesty, lying, cheating, and crooked commerce; all of these sins run rampant in this here cheaping-town. Why, if you want to know the name of the sleaziest and most fraudulent of all merchant towns, only learn this one word: Whitlee!"

Fritz looked up to the white walls and thought the man's words over. "Is it really that bad?"

"It is worse," said Reginald. His anger spent, he now went back to contemplatively smoking his pipe.

"Whitlee," Fritz repeated the name and glanced down at Florian, who shrugged, never having heard of the place before. They both turned back to the imposing gate.

Somehow they had to get inside. To detour around the city would take hours, and then they would have to find and rejoin the road on the far side, only to end up exhausted and out of doors come the inevitable nightfall.

"Excuse me, sir," said Florian, who perhaps due to his natural foxiness was the least trusting of the pair, "If you find these men so objectionable, then why do you *want* to get in their city?"

"Intelligent, yes, a very intelligent question," said Reginald, gesticulating wildly with his pipe, sending little bits of ash flying, "I took one look at you, fox, and I knew you were a bright one. Now as to why I want to get in, well that is rather a tale. You see, I have a twin sister who is at this very moment inside this witless city of Whitlee. A delicate little thing, and her name is Bijou Dumont. Poor, sweet Bijou has been arrested and is held in prison by the unscrupulous dealers for some alleged violation of their city's codes."

"You mean she broke the law?" said Fritz, trying to understand the man's strange way of speaking. He certainly used a lot of words to say very little.

"Exactly," said Reginald, "Precisely what they said!"

"Well, did she? Did she break the law?" asked Florian.

"Now that depends on who you ask, doesn't it? What happened was this: my dear sister came to this place to conduct some business, and in the process she ran afoul of some officer of the town for some made-up offense. For this, she was arrested and is being held without trial in the city. And there you have the whole reason why I desire entry into this place! Only to free my sister, and take her back home with me. To the town where honest men lay their heads, that city across the vale, that burg of wonders, that is called Goldburg. That is our home, and that is where we will go. But I must retrieve her first."

To the boy, this sounded like an honest reason, and certainly no sympathetic person could deny that it was a very good thing for a brother to be so concerned for his sister. Every sibling should show such devotion, especially to a twin, that closest of all relations.

"Maybe we could help free your sister," said Fritz, and Florian chimed in with agreement. "If you could help us get inside and through the city. You see, we are just passing through."

"Oh, I hoped you would help!" exclaimed Reginald, looking positively delighted at the boy's words, "When I saw you two gentlemen walk up, I thought to myself, 'Now, Reg, there is a pair of honest souls if ever I saw them. Those two would give their last coin to a man in need. They would give the shirt off their back. Charitable folk, they are. Generous, benevolent, caring, compassionate, why that's those two exactly!'"

Fritz and Florian smiled modestly and lowered their heads and kicked at the dirt humbly, as if to say, "Oh well, we're not all that great."

But it is a nice thing to be given such grand and high-sounding compliments by a stranger, and even level-headed adults can find all their reasonable thoughts jumbled by flattery.

"We would be happy to help," said Fritz.

"Yes, of course, we would," said Florian.

"Thank you, my new friends!" said Reginald, "Now if only this confounded curfew were off, it would be much easier to sneak into an open gate. But I guess the battle has put everyone on their guard today."

"Yes, what of that battle?" said Florian, motioning with his snout back toward the field, "Do you know anything of it? What caused it, and why?"

At each of the fox's questions, Reginald nodded his head agreeably in turn, as if he approved of them as they were put to him.

"A terrible battle, wasn't it?" he said, "I watched from just this side of the field, but I could not bear more than the initial charge. I had to leave."

"We stayed until the end," said Fritz in a solemn voice, as he thought back to all the men who had perished that day.

"The army from the south end of the field won," said Florian.

Reginald Dumont clapped his hands together and said, "Splendid! I knew they would. You see, that army comes from my home city, Goldburg, and they had, of course, the nobler side of the conflict. The men they fought are those very same scoundrels who live here in Whitlee."

"But why do they fight?" said Fritz.

"What conflict is there between Goldburg and Whitlee that it should come to such bloodshed?" said Florian.

"Why, we cannot just sit by while these evil doers thrive," said Reginald, "It is our divine duty to bring justice to them. And unfortunately sometimes the only way to deal with men so corrupt is by the sword."

Here, Reginald leaned forward, as if speaking in confidence with his newfound friends.

"And I will tell you another thing besides. The people of Whitlee are disloyal to our Queen, that noble lady who rules from the Castle in the Sky. Now how can the good men of Goldburg allow such a thing? We cannot watch idly while the scum of Whitlee thumb their noses at the Queen and stand in open rebellion against her rule."

"Is this...a civil war, then?" asked Fritz. He had heard of such things happening back home amongst certain tribes who lived in distant places, far from his parents' farm, but he had never seen one with his own eyes.

"Yes, that is it exactly! A civil war, though nothing civil about it. There are two great cities here in the Vale of Abundance, and both were once ruled peacefully from the Castle in the Sky. But no longer. Our army is made of those men loyal to the Queen. We have smashed those Whitlee fools today, and we will no doubt have to smash them again in the future."

"But didn't the army from Goldburg overrun them all today?" said Fritz, remembering the scattered army's desperate retreat. "The men were running for their lives. Won't they be captured?"

"Oh, no," said Reginald, shaking his head sadly, "The Whitlee men always flee to the Trackless Wood, which is away to the north, and hide out in that tangled place. It is impossible to find them in there. And when the Queen's army finally returns west to Goldburg, the Whitlee men creep out of their forest shelter like so many roaches from beneath a cupboard. The roaches scurry back here and hide in their city, until the time comes for another battle."

Florian shook his head and said, "But why don't you just take this city, and be done with them for good?"

"Why, it's not that easy, my foxy friend," said Reginald and pointed at the sturdy white walls,

"This city is as solid as a mountain. And the villains defend it well. We cannot break through, and so about once a year, we meet them on that open field and fight a battle. Some years, we win, and some years, the Whitlee villains win. But the war goes on. And more Whitlee children are born to replace the soldiers lost, just as more Goldburg children will grow to replace the soldiers on our side."

"But, that sounds so pointless!" said Florian.

"Yes, it doesn't seem like a very smart thing to do," said Fritz.

"My boy, no one ever said that killing each other was supposed to be smart!" said Reginald, slapping the young boy on the back good-humoredly.

"I guess that's true," said Fritz, "It just seems like a foolish way to go about it, to keep trying the same thing over and over again, year after year. And all you are doing is adding to the dead."

"Well, men die one way or another," said Reginald, "Better in raging battle than in meek old age. Better with honor than with timid disgrace."

"Yes, but shouldn't a war have an end?" said Fritz, shaking his head, "All the wars I've ever heard of have been fought and then they end, with one side the victor. A war that just goes on and on and on with no end sounds wrong."

"Ah, well, perhaps one day it will have an end," said Reginald, "But for now this is just the way it is. And who are we to question the way things are? But I say, let us focus on something more important: how we will get into the city! You see, it seems we three all have the same problem. We want into Whitlee, but the scoundrels want to keep us out."

Fritz and Florian agreed. No matter what Reginald had said about how evil the men of Whitlee were, going through this city was still the fastest way to get farther into the lands beyond.

"What do you suggest?" said Fritz.

"Here is my plan. We wait. Eventually the Whitlee soldiers who were beaten today will find their way home. And when that worthless army straggles its way back into the city, we three fall in with them, and so sneak inside amidst the crowd with no one the wiser."

Fritz considered this idea for a moment and found it to be passable. To the young boy, it seemed simple enough. If they could hide themselves in a passing cart, or walk closely next to a knight's horse and pretend to be a squire, they might be able to get past the city guards. It was worth a try at least.

"How long do you think we will have to wait?" asked Florian.

"Oh, not too long, I would imagine," said Reginald, "I do not think the Goldburg men will pursue the Whitlee soldiers much, or search for them long today. The Queen is holding a banquet for noble lords in the city of Goldburg, and many of those Goldburg knights will want to get home to be in attendance there. This will give the Whitlee cowards a chance to run home."

"Then it's a plan!" said Fritz, liking the idea more and more, "Let's wait for the army to return."

While they waited, Reginald lit his pipe again and sat blowing gentle puffs of fragrant smoke into the air. He said cheerfully to the two travelers:

"Once we free my sister, Bijou, then you two fine individuals will, of course, accompany us back to Goldburg, won't you? Perhaps we can even arrange for you to meet the Queen of the Castle in the Sky."

Fritz smiled and said, "We are going westward to seek what we may. We would love to meet the Queen of the Vale. And after that, travel even farther into the Lands Beyond the Moon."

"Oh, no," said Reginald, his face suddenly dark and grim, "You do not want to go farther than the Castle in the Sky. That is a strange, debatable and some would say, evil land to the West. There dwells the Fairy-Witch. But do not ask me any more of that now. I will not speak of her."

The small gentleman now turned his back to Fritz and Florian, and sat on his ox-cart again, looking high up at the ramparts of the walls of Whitlee. The boy and the fox looked to each other in confusion over the sudden change in his attitude. What sort of a place must that be if he would not even talk of it here in broad daylight?

So the three of them waited through a somewhat awkward silence, until Reginald's good humor returned to him. Then, the lively man talked to them excitedly about the Vale of Abundance, and some of its many comings and goings (which were trifling and unimportant and not at all worth relating here), while the trio awaited the defeated army's return.

It was not a very long wait, and it was well worth it.

Chapter 10

The first hint of the returning army was the distant sound of tramping feet. This floated in from the far north, the sullen, slogging march of many tired boots. Fritz trotted away from the city a little to get a better view, and he saw on the horizon a great throng of men trudging slowly toward the city.

There were more survivors than the young boy expected; hundreds had lived through the battle and the ensuing retreat. All showed signs of weariness or injury, or at the very least, wore a look of miserable defeat. They had lost not only a battle, but many good friends. On the faces of the men could be seen the shining tears they had wept for these fallen comrades. Their clothes were ripped and slashed in places. Rent and tattered tunics fluttered in the breeze, and splotches of mud and blood stained many coats.

There seemed to be at least a few survivors from every division of the army. Swordsmen and spearmen walked alongside the tired horses of the mounted men-at-arms. Archers walked with empty quivers, and some of the more exhausted ones dragged their long bows in the dirt as they plodded along. The heavy chargers that bore the knights were the most numerous of all. Few of these professional warriors had fallen in the battle. Some bore their own banners before them, because their young squires had been killed, probably by some stray and unlucky arrow.

In all, it was a sorry and haggard lot that marched back to Whitlee that day under the afternoon sun. As they neared the city's gate, Fritz could hear a widespread murmuring among the men. They must have been discussing the defeat because the speakers did not sound happy. Now that they were almost to the city, a voice called out from the gatehouse inside:

"Open the gate!"

And at these words, a flurry of movement began. Cords groaned and chains clinked as they tugged at the weight of the massive doors, and gears creaked and clanked as the mechanism swung open the heavy gate.

"Quick!" said Reginald, and crouched beneath the ox-cart, his face suddenly serious, "Get down. When they pass, we must find a way to fall into their ranks unnoticed."

Fritz and Florian followed his commands, scrunched down beside him, and scooted underneath the ox-cart until they were barely visible from the road. The first lines of armed men began to file past them into the city, and Fritz could now see up close how badly these men were worn down.

Some of them were actually missing limbs and had these parts tightly tied off with bloody rags. Other men wore large bandages on their head and looked barely capable of standing. It made the young boy remember the terror of the battle, and he felt sorry for these men, even if they were villains from Whitlee, as Reginald said.

After a few minutes of waiting, a creaky covered wagon rolled by, and Reginald whispered suddenly, "Go, fox! Hop aboard. It is your chance!"

Florian sprinted out from their hiding place and hopped neatly on the wagon, disappearing through its back flap in a matter of seconds. No one in the army was any the wiser. Only Fritz and Reginald had seen anything. They continued waiting until a group of knights walked by, many of them without squires, and Reginald whispered urgently to Fritz:

"Listen, boy, and follow what I say. Walk beside those knights and tell them that you were squire for another knight who fell in battle. Ask to join with one of them now."

"But what if they ask me the name of the knight I served under?" said Fritz, being a smart child and thinking ahead.

Reginald added quickly, "Say it was Sir Edmund of Vinglade. Now, go!"

Fritz nodded and trotted out into the road to fall in beside the knights.

"Hallo, good sirs!" he called up to the big men who sat sullenly on their horses, "Might I join one of you? I am afraid that my master fell in the field today."

One of the knights, a bearded and grizzled man of middle age, looked down on him with sympathy and said, "Greetings, young one. I am without a squire. You may accompany me, if you wish."

"Thank you, sir," said Fritz. The boy took the horse's reins in his hands and walked in front of him. As they passed the guard at the gate, Fritz kept his eyes lowered and his face turned away as much as possible, but this was unnecessary. There was a different guard at the gate now, and he would not have recognized the boy anyway.

They entered under the great arch and passed down a short street into a large plaza. Fritz did not look back, and he did not see how Reginald managed to get into the city, but he guessed the small gentleman had done it somehow. He surely had helped the two travelers get into Whitlee easily enough; certainly he could get himself in as well.

As Fritz and his escort walked deeper into the city of Whitlee, the middle aged knight said,

"Pray tell me, boy, what was the name of the knight you squired in this morning's battle?"

Fritz felt his face flush red hot with embarrassment, because he knew that he was about to lie. He was glad, though, that he had thought to ask Reginald for a fake name.

"Sir Edmund of Vinglade," he said, trying to make it sound like a real person.

He was surprised to hear the knight reply, "Oh, yes, Sir Edmund. I knew him well. Poor Sir Edmund! Never again will he drink the sweet wine of his ancestral land, never again will he sit at peace in his manor at Vinglade. Never, never…"

With these words, the old knight began to shed tears, and Fritz felt awful for lying this way. He had no idea that Sir Edmund *was* a real man when he used his name. Now he had just told this knight that a friend of his was dead. How terrible would it be if Sir Edmund wasn't really dead, and Fritz had made this man think he was? But then again, how much more terrible for this old knight if his friend really *was* dead!

Fritz hung his head in shame as he walked. The knight said to him, "Do not feel so bad, boy. You are young yet, and you will live to see more battles against those disgusting Goldburgers, and we will win then!"

Fritz lifted his head, but he did not tell the old knight that this was not the thing bothering him. Instead he said:

"Where are you heading now, good sir?"

The knight said, "Toward the city guard's headquarters. There are many fighting men who plan to hold a council to discuss the events of today. I wish to be there."

"Yes, sir," said Fritz, still walking.

The young boy suddenly realized that he had no idea where the city guard's headquarters were, and if he asked this knight, then the man would know that Fritz was not actually from Whitlee. What would happen to him then? Knowing the terrible things that Reginald had said about the men from Whitlee, Fritz would probably end up in chains in a dungeon cell right along with Bijou Dumont.

So Fritz walked slowly, and he was thinking anxiously about what he should do, when he heard an insistent, "*Psst! Psst!*" that drew his attention to an alley on his right. He turned and saw Reginald in his fancy green clothes, waving his arms and frantically gesturing for Fritz to come that way.

"Boy!" yelled Reginald, "Run, now!"

Before he could even think twice, Fritz followed that instruction and bolted away from the old knight. The man called out to him from atop his horse, "Hey! Where are you going?! Come back here!"

But Fritz already scurried like a rat down the alley behind the fleeing figure of Reginald Dumont. The little gentleman sure could run! Now they were fugitives in the city of Whitlee, and they ran as fast as they could to put distance between them and that knight that Fritz had abandoned. Once they got far enough away, they could blend in easily with the normal foot traffic of the bustling city.

Reginald led Fritz skillfully through the winding and narrow alley, avoiding the trash heaps and the piles of foul waste that had been dumped from windows high above. They came out suddenly on a wide avenue that was paved neatly with well-worn cobblestones.

And there was the wagon on which Florian had stowed away. It rolled slowly past them, drawn by two sluggish horses. The fox's little black nose peeked out from the dangling flap of canvas at the back of the wagon. He must have caught the scent of his friend Fritz, because he gave a quick bark and leapt out, darted away from the wagon and scampered across the avenue to join the two of them in the alley.

Now that they were all three together again, Fritz said, "What now?"

"Why, we free my sister, Bijou, of course," said Reginald, "But it will not be as easy as sneaking through the open gates of this city. These Whitlee men are evil, but they are not stupid. We will need some kind of plan if we are to get my darling sister out of their jail. And I know just the place to think of that plan!"

He pointed his finger forward and walked purposefully out into the street, leading Fritz and Florian. As the fox and the boy followed, Florian said:

"Where is that exactly?"

"A tavern, my foxy friend!" said Reginald with a broad smile and a mischievous wink, "A tall tankard of ale always helps me think better!"

Florian cast a doubtful look at Fritz, but the two travelers followed the small gentleman who had somehow become their leader. Reginald walked with knowledgeable ease through the winding streets of the city. He had obviously been here many times, for he never paused at the intersections but hurried through them like a dog on a strong scent.

The place to which he led them was a rickety building, the architectural equivalent of a pair of trousers that has been torn and patched too many times. Boards of odd colors had been nailed up to replace parts of the wall, and the whole thing was a mess of spots that had been repaired and spots that awaited repair. The whole building seemed to lean heavily to one side, as some of its patrons were also doing when they walked out of it, and the name on the sign out front was quite appropriate.

The tavern was called, "The Tilted Tankard."

As Reginald, Fritz and Florian pushed their way through the doors into the shadowy place, they could see little but the vague outlines of men scattered throughout the bar. The brightness of the afternoon sun outside left the trio unable to see for many long seconds until their eyes adjusted. When the inside finally came into focus, Reginald raised his hand, caught the eye of the barkeep, and called out:

"Ho, there! Roger! My good man! I say, a tankard of your finest brew!"

The man named Roger was a burly, barrel-chested oaf who looked like he could carry several kegs of beer singlehandedly. His forearms were like tree trunks and covered in heavy black hair, his face hidden behind a heavy beard. He glowered at Reginald from behind the bar and said harshly:

"You little shyster. You've a lot of nerve coming in here."

Reginald shook his head, chuckling, and waved a hand to Fritz and Florian. He whispered over his shoulder:

"That's just how Roger is. You two have a seat over there. I will speak to him."

Fritz nodded, and he and Florian went to a table in the dim back corner, away from the other patrons of the tavern, who looked like rather unsavory characters. When the boy and the fox were alone, Florian said:

"I'm not sure I like this place."

"I know I don't," said Fritz, "It's an ugly sort of place, isn't it? A place that serves ugly sorts of drinks to ugly sorts of people."

Fritz had again unknowingly spoke the truth as only a child can, but likewise, he failed to see the significance of his statement. He was not thinking of Reginald at all when he said it, but of the other rough-looking men who sat hunched and dirty over their stiff drinks.

Yet his mind did not linger on the bar. Soon he was thinking of the bigger picture, pondering again the ongoing war between Goldburg and Whitlee. Hanna had said there would be unrest in this valley. When he mentioned this to Florian, the fox said:

"Yes, it does seem like an awful situation. To send so many young men off to die year after year."

"Do you think that Hanna meant we were supposed to put an end to it? She did say that we were supposed to help these people out of evil."

"She did," agreed Florian, thoughtfully, "But how can we two end such a deep-rooted conflict?"

"I suppose we start by helping to free Bijou," said Fritz, "Then, when we get to Goldburg, we can find out more from there."

"Perhaps," said Florian, casting an uncertain glance at Reginald Dumont, who gulped large mouthfuls of frothy ale at the bar.

"For all his high-sounding talk about the scoundrels of Whitlee, our gentleman Dumont seems to fit in quite well here."

Fritz nodded, but he was not really listening to Florian. His mind was on the city and the things that he had seen in the streets. There had been kind-faced women walking hand-in-hand with their neatly-dressed daughters who had their hair styled in cute ringlets that fell happily on their little shoulders. There had been somber-faced men wearing the clothing of farmers and haymakers who seemed to been walking out of the city to return to their country homes now that the danger of battle had passed. In the markets that had opened, there were people of all kinds, buying and selling and inspecting goods, and haggling and bargaining over this and that.

In short, there had been in the streets of Whitlee all the things one expected to find in a city of normal, lawful people. There was nothing anywhere to indicate that they were crooked, low-down villains as Reginald had described them. Fritz was puzzled by this and did not know what to make of it.

He did not have a chance to come to a conclusion either, because at that moment, Reginald Dumont made a sudden appearance at their little table. He slammed his pewter cup roughly on the wood and sloshed a wave of ale over the brim. He laughed at the splashing brew and said with a voice that smelled heavily of suds:

"My friends, I have a plan!"

Chapter 11

The plan to free Bijou Dumont was not much of a plan:

"Here it is. We three are a traveling troupe of entertainers," said Reginald with a hiccup and a chuckle, "A merry band of jugglers, jokesters…" and with a wink to Florian, "and…and animal performers! Ha ha! We come to the door of the keep, that is, the prison of Whitlee…"

Here, Reginald sank into a chorus of irrepressible giggles, as if utterly pleased with his idea. After a few moments, the small gentleman regained his composure.

"I say, we come to the door in our disguises. I will be the leader, of course, and Fritz, m'boy, you will be my sidekick and Florian will be our trick animal. Now, there will be two guards on duty at the outer door to the prison. We bluff our way past them into the mess hall of the keep with promises of a free show for the guards on duty. There are always minstrels and court jesters and other various performers who entertain the guards. The men of Whitlee are used to it, and I don't doubt they will accept us. This will allow us to gain entry into the prison."

"But will we have to give a show?" said Fritz nervously.

"Oh, m'boy," said Reginald after downing another mouthful of ale and raising his hand for more, "I've put on many shows in my lifetime, and I can tell you it is a breeze. Just follow my lead. Y'know, I used to actually be in a troupe, once upon a time. My sister, too. A great big traveling troupe made up of folk of all sorts. We wheeled around in a wondrous wagon painted with wild colors and full of marvels and magic."

Fritz smiled despite the growing drunkenness of the small gentleman. He had always been fascinated by the traveling folk who occasionally passed by his parents' farm in their brightly painted wooden-sided wagons. The boy's wide eyes lit up even more when Reginald added:

"Real magic, too! Not mere stage tricks, I tell you, but genuine, authentic magic!"

"Can you do magic?" asked Fritz.

"No, no, not me," said Reginald, "But Bijou, oh my, she is a magical one indeed!"

Florian squinted in doubt. But whatever his doubts might have been about the magical abilities of the prisoner, the fox still seemed willing to help with her escape.

"What do we do once we reach your sister inside the prison?" said Florian, "How will we get out unnoticed?"

"Ah ha! Now, that is the trick, isn't it?" said Reginald very loudly, spitting little flecks of foam. "We shall see. We shall see what my dear old Bijou has up her sleeves, ha ha! Up her sleeves!"

Florian did not look entirely satisfied with this answer, but Fritz said, "We should go right away. If we are to free her, I want to do it soon and get out of this city as quickly as we can. I don't want to stay in Whitlee if the men are all criminals."

The boy was looking at the bartender who frowned in their direction. The bartender eyed Reginald and his two companions with growing disapproval, and Fritz felt extremely out of place in this dimly lit tavern.

"Hallo!" yelled out the bartender finally, "Reginald Dumont, you get your sorry drunken carcass out of my establishment! Take your lies elsewhere."

"Can you believe this?" said Reginald to the boy and the fox, jerking a thumb in the man's direction, "Whitlee scum insulting me, an honorable chap from Goldburg? Well, now you see how inhospitable and hostile and downright mean these villains are. Let's go!"

Reginald led Fritz and Florian out of the tavern quickly, and it was a good thing he chose that moment to make an exit, because a large mug of ale came soaring and splattered against the door just as it closed behind them.

Outside, Reginald squinted in the sunlight and let out a loud, obnoxious burp.

"Their swill is a sorry excuse for proper ale anyway," said Dumont. Then, he turned this way and that as if trying to get his bearings, and recognizing the direction, he pointed his finger and walked forward with quick steps. Fritz and Florian hurried after him, the fox's patience for the eccentric and boisterous man growing thin.

As they walked, Florian made his doubts known.

"How will we get past the guards when we don't look a thing like performers?"

Reginald waved away the question and said, "No problem! You just let me do the talking. I have no doubt they will buy my story."

Florian gave a skeptical shrug, but Fritz tried to put aside his own doubt about the escapade. That is, until they neared the prison and a thought suddenly struck him.

"Mister Dumont, you said your sister was magical. If that is so, then why does she not just use her magic to free herself?"

Reginald turned with a grin on his face and said, "But you are a smart one, aren't you! And yes, she is magical, very magical indeed, but there is something peculiarly powerful about a locked jail cell. Something that puzzles many a magical mind, except for perhaps the most supremely gifted of sorcerers. A lock is a powerful piece of magic. I fear she cannot break out on her own, no, not from inside a locked door."

This made sense to Fritz, though he had never thought about a lock being magical. Reginald Dumont, except for his taste for ale, seemed to the boy such a knowledgeable and friendly man that it did not quite enter Fritz's mind to mistrust him. And any mistrust that might have been was completely erased by the thought of poor Bijou locked in a dark cell. Fritz just had to help free the sweet girl.

He and Florian followed Reginald boldly up to the front door of the prison keep, a single tall tower of stone with only a few narrow windows near the top. The entrance was an arched double door made of heavy iron, bolted fast, and directly on either side of this stood two imposing men-at-arms. Each of these men had their faces covered by iron helmets and in their hands, they gripped a sinister-looking halberd.

"What business have you at the prison?" asked one of the guards in a stern voice, though Fritz could not tell which of the men had spoken because neither had moved their lips an inch. In fact, they stood so still that they seemed to be statues.

"My good man," said Reginald, placing his hand on his belly and bowing low in humble greeting, "We are but three traveling performers, and we come to offer a free show to the men here in appreciation of their services to this fine city."

The guards still did not move, but one of them said in a tone of disbelief, "You three are performers?"

"Indeed!" replied Reginald quickly. Pulling Fritz forward and holding him by the shoulders, he said:

"This here is my young boy, Fritz, a juggler of extraordinary talent! Not only that, but he is a...a fire eater, lion wrestler and fortune teller, and can perform many other strange and interesting, dazzling and daring deeds."

This fine introduction made Fritz blush, not least because it was a total lie; the young boy knew that he could do none of those things. What's more, Reginald made Fritz sound like the boy was his son.

When Reginald motioned for Florian, the fox stepped forward and the man said, "And this is the Fantastic Florian, the fox of fabulous and far-fetched feats that will flummox and floor you. Death defying leaps through flaming rings, delicate balancing acts on a tightrope over a pit of spears, and many other marvels sure to amuse and awe the men of this fine prison."

Through both of these bombastic speeches, the guards had not even turned their heads and had shown no interest in Reginald. Yet when he was finished speaking, after a few moments of awkward silence during which Fritz worried the scheme would fail, the guards suddenly stepped aside and threw open the door.

"You will find the men in the mess hall," said the voice of the guard, "Proceed down these stairs and tell the captain what you told us. A show will be a nice treat for the men, especially after the news from the battlefield earlier."

Fritz and Florian entered first, followed by Reginald, who they could hear behind them uttering things to the guards such as, "Oh, yes, wasn't that a terrible battle? Just awful. Absolutely awful. So many good men lost. So many fine young lads that will never come home. Just terrible…"

As Fritz walked down the stairs, he wondered how this small gentleman could lie with such little regard to the truth and how he could do it so effortlessly. Just minutes ago Reginald had denounced all Whitlee men as scoundrels and villains, and now he was praising their exploits on the battlefield and lamenting their deaths.

Even Fritz was beginning to think poorly of this slick and fast-talking little man, although the boy's commitment to freeing his poor imprisoned sister had not changed. Surely Bijou deserved freedom, even if her brother was a little obnoxious (and a little drunk, too). And Reginald *had* helped them get into the city and promised to lead them farther west.

So Fritz tried to push away any doubts he had as they entered the prison. They had come this far, and it was too late to back out now.

The stairs came out on a dimly lit hallway that flickered with the flames of torches that lined the stone walls, perched in their iron sconces. Down this hall, the trio walked until they came to a wide mess hall with three huge banquet tables to serve the guardsmen. Many guards already sat on the long benches on either side of these tables, hunched over some stew that steamed in wooden bowls in front of them. A rowdy and loud chatter filled the room, the talk of a hundred men who knew each other well and enjoyed each other's company.

One man stood at the end of a table, and he wore the bright badge of the Captain of the Guard upon the outer cloak that draped over his iron chest plate. He was a stout man with wide shoulders and arms that looked like they could swing an axe hard enough to fell a tree in a single swipe. At his belt dangled a huge ring of iron keys.

Reginald approached this man and said, "Hail, captain, and greetings! I am Reginald of the Roving Band of Revelers! We are a humble band of performers, come this day to entertain you and your men with a complimentary show."

The captain looked Reginald up and down, and then turned his hard gaze upon Fritz and Florian. After a steely silence, the captain said:

"Aye, you may give us a show. Providing it is free. And don't be expecting tips neither."

"We live only to entertain, my good captain," said Reginald, pretending to be slightly insulted, "Your laughter is all the payment we desire!"

With a quick wink to his two accomplices, the small gentleman leapt on the table, almost knocked over a bowl of stew, and shouted:

"Hallo! You men of Whitlee! Your attention, please! The Roving Band of Revelers is here to entertain you! Look here and prepare to be amazed by wondrous works of performing art. Allow me to introduce my two companions: Fritz the Boy Wonder, fire eater, lion wrestler, fortune teller and sword juggler of such splendid skill as to surprise and startle such spectators as you sirs! And the Fantastic Florian, that flamboyant fox of flash and flair. Never again will you see two so talented. This is the show of a lifetime, one that you will not soon forget."

Fritz could not help but notice that he had gained another talent in the repeating of Reginald's speech. He wondered how the man expected him to back up these claims. Fritz had never eaten fire before, and he had certainly never wrestled a lion; he had never even seen a lion!

Reginald seemed fearless and unconcerned about such matters though, as he leapt down from the table, all the eyes of the mess hall now focused squarely on him. He turned his back to his audience and addressed Fritz and Florian in a hushed voice. He looked straight into Fritz's eyes with a look that the boy had never seen before and said:

"Now, instead, I'll give them a show they *will* forget. You just follow my lead. And you, too, fox. Ha ha! Hey hey! They'll soon forget this wondrous day!"

As Reginald Dumont spoke, his voice became more song-like and melodious, and his tone and the things he said turned to near whispers that tickled Fritz and Florian's ears. They were drawn in, and Fritz began to have a strange, sleepy feeling as the small man chanted and sang.

Fritz could not have said what the words were exactly, and many years later, he remembered only the uncanny feeling created by rhymed lines about many marveled things. The power in the man's voice twisted around the two travelers and bound them up as easily as if his words were rope.

At some point, Fritz forgot that he stood in the mess hall of a prison, and he felt as if he were sleeping quite soundly on a floating cloud. He knew that Reginald had turned again to address the guards, but the young boy was completely lost in his own mind. Something in Reginald's voice threw its power over the guard's ears, too.

Fritz remembered little else, except a descending fog that swallowed up all of his thoughts. He and Florian must have performed some sort of feat to wow the guards, because they were not arrested. And Fritz faintly remembered cheering crowds and the clapping of wild applause, but they were like the half-forgotten sensations that one feels in a dream.

The next thing that Fritz knew for sure, he and Florian stood in a dark hallway with cells receding in front them on either side of the corridor. In the young boy's hand, he clutched tightly the ring of keys that had been on the captain's belt earlier.

Then, he heard the desperate voice of a woman call out:

"What are you waiting for? Get me out of here!"

Chapter 12

The voice belonged to Bijou Dumont, of course, and she stood inside the cell to Fritz's left.

She was a small woman, though a little taller than her brother. There was some peculiar quality about her that roused uneasiness in Fritz in that split second when he first saw her. What it was, he could not say; nothing particular stood out as its source.

The little woman was much more attractive than Reginald. Her face was shapely, the features round and soft, and large attractive eyes held the two travelers in their gaze. She was simply dressed, as prisoners usually are; she wore a plain white tunic, somewhat stained around the bottom from the dirt and grime of long wear. Her delicate hands held the iron door of her cell and her face was framed between the bars.

"Please, you must hurry," she said, "You haven't much time now."

Fritz shook his head, somewhat puzzled and dazed still, as one who has been suddenly awoken from a deep sleep. He looked at the fox and saw the same look of confusion mirrored in Florian's face.

"How did we..." began the boy, "I mean, what—"

"No time, no time," said Bijou Dumont, excitedly shaking at the bars which did not budge an inch, "There is no time now. You are here, and you have the keys. Unlock the door!"

Fritz looked down at the large iron ring in his hand. There must have been over a hundred jingling keys on it.

"But which one goes to this door?" said the boy.

"That one," said Bijou, and pointed to a dull, chipped key that looked like it had opened many locks, "That one, there! I'm sure of it. Now, hurry."

Fritz fumbled with the key ring for a moment, got the right key in his hand and pushed it into the lock. With a creaking of the mechanism, he turned the key, and suddenly the prison cell door swung open.

In one swift, silent motion, Bijou Dumont leapt gracefully into the hall, her white tunic flowing behind her.

"Ha ha!" she shouted in triumph, "I am free!"

Fritz smiled, happy that they had helped liberate the poor, sweet woman. Yet he also still felt like his head was swimming in a lingering fog. How had he and Florian gotten down into

138

the depths of the prison, and how had they come by the keys of the Captain of the Guard?

And where was Reginald Dumont, that wily, silver-tongued little man?

The answer to this last question soon became clear, because the small gentleman came running headlong down the dungeon corridor, waving his arms frantically over his head.

"Run!" shouted Reginald, as he barreled down the hall toward the others, "Quickly, now, be gone! The whole of the city guard is upon us!"

Fritz's heart jumped into his throat and began pounding out a steady rhythm. His puzzlement over how he and Florian had gotten from the fake performance into the belly of the prison was quickly forgotten. All he could think of now was a hundred armed guardsmen coming for them. Surely they would be caught. There was no way out. They would be arrested…or maybe worse.

"What will we do?" said the boy.

"Yes, you had a plan for getting us in," said Florian, his wits returning to him just then, "What about a plan for getting us out?"

"Hush!" said Reginald, pushing them on down the hall, "Be quiet and follow. Bijou, my dear sister, you know what to do!"

Fritz did not know what that meant, but Bijou seemed to understand perfectly. She hurried away down the corridor, away from the sound of the shouting guards that could be heard clambering down the stairs. Reginald pushed Fritz and Florian to follow, and follow they did.

Bijou apparently knew these prison hallways well, and Fritz began to wonder if this was not her first time in them. What sort of people were these siblings Dumont after all? But he had no time to decide just now, because the guards were closing in. When he looked back over his shoulder, Fritz saw the gleaming of drawn swords in the flickering torchlight.

"Faster!" shouted Reginald.

Bijou said nothing, but turned this way and that as the hallways snaked around and split off and went up and down flights of stairs. Fritz would have been utterly lost in such a maze-like building, but Bijou never thought twice, never hesitated, not even for a second, never missed a step as she picked out the way.

Finally, she turned a corner and was lost from sight for a moment. When the other three rounded the corner, they saw the little woman above them, bounding up a long flight of spiral stairs, taking the steps two or three at a time.

"Up we go!" said Reginald.

The guards were almost upon them, and Fritz heard the clanking of steel and the pounding of booted feet and the shouts of "Stop!" and "We'll get you scoundrels!"

The boy and the fox scampered up the stairs as fast as their little feet and little paws could carry them. Higher and higher the stairs went, winding and winding, up and up, until Fritz realized that they must even now be scaling the entire height of the high tower. But what good would it do to climb the tower? Would they not be trapped at the top with no way down? Would the guards not catch them in the end?

Fritz worried, but he and Florian had no choice but to follow the Dumonts. The travelers had gotten themselves too deeply involved in this escapade to just stop running. Somehow the boy did not think the guards would be very sympathetic if he just gave himself up. And he would never go farther into the Lands Beyond the Moon if that happened.

So he ran on, as tired as he was, up the long flight of stairs. Finally, they reached the top and Bijou threw open the door onto the tower's roof. The bright sunlight flooded in with a burst of rays, and Fritz blinked his eyes in the stark light.

When they were all out, Reginald slammed the door shut behind them, but Fritz knew that it would not hold off the guards for long. The boy saw exactly what he had feared. They stood on a wide, circular roof, and although Fritz could see the whole city of Whitlee laid out below him like a living map, he could see no way down.

They were trapped.

Or at least, they would have been trapped, had it been only Fritz and Florian on that rooftop.

Neither of those two knew any magic (thankfully, for it is a dark and sinful thing), but they had forgotten what Reginald said about his sister.

"She is a magical one, indeed!"

The woman had a plan all along. As Fritz and Florian watched in bewilderment, Bijou Dumont produced from within her plain white tunic, a single black feather. It looked to be the feather of a raven, a long, glossy jet-colored feather that shimmered in the sun. She held this feather aloft and said words that Fritz had never heard before, an eerie, unsettling language. Even though he knew not the meaning, the words gave him goosebumps and sent a shiver down his back.

Then, something incredible happened.

Just as the guards burst through the door behind them, Bijou cried, "Grab hold of my tunic!"

Fritz and Florian, as frightened as they were, followed her instruction. Fritz took a handful of the garment and Florian closed his foxy teeth on a piece as well. Reginald took hold, too.

Bijou walked to the edge of the tower, and at the very moment when the guards reached out to grab hold of them, she leapt from the building, taking the other three with her.

Fritz felt terror for a second, though nowhere near as strongly as the terror he'd felt when the Shadow chased them through the Mountains of the Moon. His stomach turned somersaults as the bottom of the world fell out from under him. The terror was brief, because he did not plummet to his death as he had feared. When he looked around to see how this could be, he received a different kind of shock.

Bijou Dumont had sprouted huge, black wings where her arms had been. She held these wings straight out to either side, gliding gracefully through the air with the other three clutching tightly to her. Behind them on the tower, the guards shouted and shook their fists at the escapees.

Reginald laughed and shouted back, "So long! Farewell, you foul fools of this festering city! You will never hold the Dumonts! Ha ha!"

Fritz said nothing, still marveling at the means of their escape, and Florian *could not* say anything, because if he opened his mouth, he would surely fall.

The feathers of Bijou's arms fluttered in the brisk air, as the group flew over the city of Whitlee, as easily as the birds of the sky. The city passed beneath them like water under a bridge, flowing by in a flurry of colors and smells and sounds, and soon enough they soared beyond the outer wall. The roads and alleys and buildings turned suddenly to dirt paths and green fields and the tops of red and yellow and orange trees.

In this strange way, the four of them left behind the city of Whitlee and covered many miles and miles of open land. As if on a sea of green, capped here and there with the dark breakers of trees, the sailors traveled lightly, borne on by the black sails of Bijou's magical arms.

Never once did she flap her black wings, but held them steady, letting the rushing wind bear her and her passengers on their way west. Fritz turned his head this way and that, to see the Lands Beyond the Moon stretched out beneath him.

Far, far away to the north, he could see dimly the stretches of what must be the Trackless Wood, as Reginald had called it, unending treetops cascading away into the vast distance. To the south, he could see, just before the curve of the horizon faded out of sight, a strange expanse of beige, a kind of land for which the young boy had no name, for he had never seen, or imagined, such a thing as a desert.

But when he looked ahead to the West, he could see nothing very different from the land they were soaring over now. It was all green, or different shades of green, as far as his eyes reached. He had thought to catch a glimpse of the Castle in the Sky, but it must be far away yet, because there was not a hint of it on that far horizon.

Reginald's voice interrupted his thoughts.

"What an escape!" said the man, chuckling to himself, with breath that still smelled faintly of ale, "I say, it was perfectly executed! Why, if you two are not the best couple of jailbreakers that I've ever recruited…You did fine, just fine!"

Florian tried to reply with something, but because the fox could still not open his mouth to speak, all that came out were unintelligible grunts and growls.

Fritz, however, shook his head and said, "I don't remember a thing! How did we end up with the keys? And how did we get to your sister's cell? The last thing I remember you were starting the show…"

"Ah ha! But you are not supposed to remember anything after that," said Reginald with mischief in his eyes, "Just be happy that we got out of that scrape alive!"

Fritz *was* happy for that fact, happier than he could have said, but he was not very satisfied with this strange gentleman's answers. In fact, he was beginning to be rather unhappy to have ever met Reginald Dumont at all. The man's way of speaking was beginning to irritate the boy, and Fritz thought now that Reginald and his sister may not be at all what they had first seemed.

This business with making them forget made Fritz very suspicious. Even still, he could not abandon the two Dumont siblings just yet. For one thing, if he and Florian tried to right now, they would fall to their deaths. And for another, they seemed the quickest way to reach Goldburg.

Maybe then, he and Florian could bid farewell to these strangers.

Fritz noticed that they were losing altitude, almost as if the wind were going out of their sails, that is to say, out of Bijou's dark feathers. The ground was rising up to meet them ever so slowly.

"We're coming down," he said to the others.

"Yes, yes, we are, my observant friend," said Reginald. Then, the man pointed forward to a snaking line that divided the land neatly into two and said:

"See there, that is the Rushing River, the very same water that we left so far away on the other side of Whitlee. Now it curves back around, and serves as the official border between the lands of Whitlee and the lands of Goldburg."

On this side of the river were the flatlands of the Vale, lands suitable for farming and for grazing herds, open lands shaded in spots by bunches of trees. Yet the closer the land came to the river, the more abundant these trees became. They never quite came together to make a forest, however, not until the other side of the river. There they became a dense tangle of dark green wood that stretched away unbroken toward the West.

As the company flew on in that direction, they sank lower and lower in the sky, and Fritz said, "I don't think we're going to reach the river. We're going to come down long before then."

"Well, what do you want?" said Bijou suddenly in annoyance, "I am doing my best! But I am only a weak magician. I have neither the sorcery of the Queen nor the more dreadful power of that Fairy-Witch who lives beyond the Ditch of Wyrms."

"Who is she?" said Fritz in a small voice, for this was the second time the Fairy-Witch had been mentioned.

"A terrible enemy to us," said Reginald, "And a terrible enemy to our Queen of the Castle in the Sky. It is the Fairy-Witch who is the root of discord and strife in the Vale."

"Oh," was all Fritz could say.

"Yes, oh, indeed!" said Reginald, "And I am afraid that is not the last you shall hear of her. But look! We are touching down."

And so they were.

Chapter 13

The ground met them gently and caught them on a cushion of green grass and loamy earth. Springy and supple, the blades of grass bent under them and cradled them as they plopped down in a tumbling bundle of bodies. Fritz and Florian rolled away from the other two, who came down with practiced ease on their feet. They undoubtedly had flown before. They executed their landing as effortlessly as real birds.

Fritz and Florian picked themselves up and dusted bits of grass and twigs and leaves out of their hair and fur. It was not easy to make such a practiced landing when you've lived your whole life on solid ground.

The group had touched down still in the lands of Whitlee on a wide plain that was sprinkled with trees. Not a house could be seen anywhere, not a farm, not a fence, not a single bit of civilization. They were in the empty borderlands between the two city-states.

"Well, I guess we should start walking," said Fritz, pointing to the West.

"Right you are, my boy!" said Reginald, still annoyingly energetic and cheerful.

Now that Florian could speak without having to hold on for dear life with his teeth, the fox said, "How long of a walk is it? I was hoping you would fly us all the way to Goldburg."

Bijou replied in a voice whose annoyance had grown almost to anger:

"Will you listen to that? I fly them out of danger and certain death, and what do they say? You didn't fly us far enough! What, do you think magicians just snap their fingers and the thing is so? Well, let me tell you something, that little flight took a lot of my energy. I nearly spent myself completely getting us this far, carrying your sorry bodies like so much dead weight. You would think the least that I would get is gratitude. A little thanks perhaps!"

She shook herself suddenly, and there was a quick *poof!* The black feathers were all gone. A fairly normal set of female arms reappeared in their proper place.

"I am sorry for my friend," said Fritz, hoping to avoid unpleasantness. Florian, for his part, did not look a bit sorry, and not at all like he was about to thank Bijou. In fact, he looked almost as angry as she was. Fritz added quickly:

"We *are* very thankful!"

"Yes, well, there you have it," said Reginald, and patting Fritz on the shoulder, he added, "Let us be off. In answer to your question, fox, it is a rather long walk, I'm afraid. But we should make it in about a day or so."

So the four of them headed off west. When they had gone a little way, Florian hung back from the Dumonts and motioned for Fritz to join him. They ambled along and let the siblings get farther ahead. When those two were out of earshot, Florian whispered to the boy:

"I am growing suspicious of those two. I was always taught to be wary of folk who could change form. Shapeshifters are an evil lot."

"Oh, I don't think she is a shapeshifter," said Fritz, scratching his head, "That was just a stage trick. She's a performing magician."

"Some stage trick!" said Florian, "That was no illusion, flying us of the city that way. And what about Reginald and that honey tongue of his? I believe he bewitched us, the same as he did the guards. No, I do not like that one bit…"

"Well, we made it through Whitlee, didn't we?" said Fritz, trying to convince himself as much as Florian, "And we're headed west, just like we wanted. Reginald said he might even introduce us to their Queen. So even though we don't like them, I think the best thing to do is go at least as far as Goldburg with them."

"Maybe you are right," said Florian, squinting at the figures ahead of them, "I hope you are."

Up ahead, Reginald half-turned and said over his shoulder, "Hurry up you two! You will not make the trip any shorter by lagging behind!"

"Come on, Florian," said the boy and trotted to catch up. The fox followed his young friend. Florian did not speak anymore of his suspicion, but he knew that if it came to it, he would do whatever it took to defend Fritz. The young boy would do no less for his friend.

On and on walked their odd little company, passing through the open, unsettled countryside of the great green valley. Although there were no houses or cottages nearby, the lands were not wholly uninhabited. The travelers passed many rabbits and squirrels and fawns that went scampering off at the sound of the tramping strangers. Overhead, flitting from branch to branch, half-concealed in the leaves, were dozens of birds of all kinds: swifts and swallows and wrens and thrushes and warbles, to name a few.

None of these animals came close or lingered long when they saw the travelers, and the creatures showed either no ability or no desire to speak with them. The Dumonts did not even take notice of them; those two walked straight west and paid very little attention to anything around them. But Fritz and Florian noticed all the woodland animals, and the fox whispered that he thought it strange not one had learned to speak.

Soon, however, they came upon something that even the Dumont siblings could not ignore. Ahead of them grew a grove of tall beech trees, and beneath the smooth-barked trees, clustered in the deep shadows of their shade, stood a group of formidable-looking horses.

At first, Fritz thought that they had merely stumbled upon another group of travelers, perhaps resting their mounts for a moment beneath the shelter of the tall trees. But as he walked closer, the boy could see that the horses had no riders; indeed, there were no saddles or gear of any kind to be seen and certainly no sign that anyone owned the horses.

Rather the herd milled about on their own, standing roughly in a semi-circle around a beautiful stallion of the purest silver hair. As Fritz got closer, it was clear to him from their demeanor that these animals were wild. An unspeakable majesty surrounded them, and their manner and the blaze of their shining eyes told him that they had never known anything but the complete freedom of an untamed life.

Reginald and Bijou came to a halt, and they were obviously unsure what to make of the herd. The wild horses were quite large, and the Dumont siblings seemed wary of approaching them.

"Do you think they can speak?" said Florian.

"I haven't the faintest idea, my foxy fellow," said Reginald, "But if they live in the lands of Whitlee, I am not sure they will be friendly to us."

"Shouldn't we at least introduce ourselves?" said Fritz, thinking it rude to just stand here talking about them. It was true that the wild horses had not seen them yet, but that made the boy feel even more poorly mannered to be watching someone without their knowledge.

"Yes, let's go say hallo," said Florian and trotted suddenly forward. Fritz followed, and the Dumonts had no choice but to reluctantly join them. As he neared the grove of gray-barked beeches, Fritz called out:

"Hallo and greetings!"

He did not want to bound into the shaded grove and startle such powerful beasts. As it was, he still seemed to give the horses quite a start. A couple of them reared up in surprise and whinnied and neighed wildly.

The silver stallion stepped forward with a stern face and said, "Who are you who dare to so boldly interrupt the War Council of Wild Horses?"

"Your pardons, please," said Fritz and bowed his head in respect to the splendid animal, "We are only travelers headed west, and we did not know this was a council."

"A *war* council," said a handsome paint horse, a brown animal speckled and flecked here and there with white hair.

"Are you at war?" said the young boy, as he turned to all the wild horses one by one. Besides the silver stallion and the paint, there were two deep chestnut-colored horses, a gray, and a horse as black as a starless night.

The gray spoke and said, "Of course we are at war."

The silver said, "We are loyal animals, and thus we will be at war until that so-called Queen is thrown down from the Castle in the Sky."

Fritz noticed that the Dumonts sank quietly back from the grove. Soon, the two had gone out of earshot. But Fritz felt no fear from the wild horses; he and Florian were not, after all, loyal to any one side in this civil war. The horses did not seem to wish them harm either. The silver stallion only seemed curious about who they were.

"Why do you travel west?" he said, "That land is held by the enemy, though it was once a lovely part of this Vale."

Fritz thought it unwise to say anything of the Dumonts of Goldburg, or to reveal that he had helped Bijou break out of prison in Whitlee, so he told another part of the truth.

"My name is Fritz," he said, "And I have crossed the Milky Way and journeyed over the Mountains of the Moon. This is my friend,

Florian, who I met in those same mountains. We were seeking the horizon, when we met the shepherdess Hanna. She told us our destiny lay in the West, far into the Lands Beyond the Moon, and that we were to bring an end to evil there."

When he finished, the wild horses wondered greatly at his words, and there was much whinnying and neighing and stamping of hooves. After the commotion fell away, the huge silver stallion knelt in front of the boy as one showing respect.

"If what you speak is true, and you are friends of that golden-haired maiden, know this," said the horse, "You and this fox will forever be our friends as well, and we will do all we can to help you along."

Fritz was very happy to hear this, although he felt a little dishonest for not telling the silver stallion about the Dumonts. Yet the animal seemed to guess at the two strangers who kept their distance beyond the edge of the grove.

"Those two yonder," said the stallion and nodded at the Dumonts, "They carry the look of Goldburg about them. If they be your fellow travelers, then be wary and keep your wits about you. The shepherdess Hanna may not have warned you, but all is not always as it seems in the Lands Beyond the Moon."

Florian nodded as if thinking, "I knew it."

Fritz simply said, "Thank you for the advice. We must go on now, into the distant West."

The silver stallion agreed, and he signaled for the other wild horses to stand aside. Fritz waved to Reginald and Bijou, who hurried through the grove with their heads down, not daring to make eye contact with the imposing animals. A couple of snorts sounded in the grove as the Dumonts passed, but the wild horses did not hinder the two.

When the four travelers had walked a mile beyond the beech grove, Reginald exclaimed, "My boy, whatever did you say to those beastly brutes that they allowed us to pass through? I say, I thought we were done for! I have seen such horses trample a man as easily as a fallen leaf, indeed I have!"

Fritz did not answer the man, and Florian said nothing as well. The blessing of the shepherdess did not need to be shared with this smooth-talking man and his uncanny sister. Fritz hoped they would reach Goldburg soon. He did not care for the company of the Dumonts anymore.

At least they had already reached the border between the lands of Whitlee and Goldburg.

The Rushing River flowed before them.

Chapter 14

There was no bridge over the churning white water.

On the opposite bank, the dark green forest, which Fritz had seen from the air, sprang up and stretched away into the shadowed distance. But there was no road, no way to reach the far side.

"How will we get across?" said Fritz.

"Well, don't look at me," said Bijou, shrugging her shoulders and twirling the raven's feather between her fingers, "I am tired yet from flying. I haven't any more magic right now, so do not ask me!"

Florian shook his head and mumbled to himself, "We were not going to."

Reginald produced his pipe, sat down cross-legged on the soft ground and set about lighting up. When he got the bowl smoking, he took a breath, spouted a puff and said:

"Ah, but it is a difficult conundrum, isn't it? Hmm…"

Then, he trailed off into contemplative smoking. Florian the fox did not seem so content to just sit and wait for something to happen, however, and Fritz was glad for his friend then.

"I think we ought to just swim," said Florian, "There is no sense in sitting idly on the bank. Where is that going to get us?"

Fritz smiled and said, "I am up for swimming."

After all, this Rushing River was no wider than the Milky Way, and Fritz had splashed his way through that mystifying water easily enough. Of course, this river flowed much more quickly and with more force than the starry stream, but Fritz, with the supreme confidence of a young boy, felt sure that he could brave these rapids.

"Let's swim it," he said and stepped to the very edge of the river.

Reginald waved his hand and said, "Wait, now! Just you wait."

"I do not wish to drown here," said Bijou, scowling at the river.

"Drown?" said Florian, scowling at Bijou in turn, "How can you drown if you are such a magician?"

"If that was meant to mock my powers, you foxy fool, then I will have you know that I only use magic when I *have* to. I do not think this qualifies as one of those times."

"Well, I think it does!" said Florian, obviously fed up with the Dumont woman. With that, the fox leapt into the Rushing River and disappeared beneath the foamy waters with a *plosh!*

Fritz laughed and followed with an even bigger *bloop!*

Soon both of the companions surfaced, their heads bobbing up and down in the swift current, their arms straining against the water. Although the current tugged them downstream, both the fox and the young boy made it across to the far bank.

Reginald and Bijou sighed in annoyance, but having no other choice, the siblings jumped into the cool water. They had a much harder go of it. Neither one of them was a very good swimmer, and a silver tongue does not help you much in a churning river; you cannot talk your way out of a drowning. As it was, the pair came up sputtering and coughing and managed to reach the bank, although they came out of the water much farther downstream.

All four had reached the west side, however, and that was something. Now they could continue their journey. Fritz wrung out his wet sleeves, and Florian shook the beads of cool mountain water from his orange fur. Reginald and Bijou rejoined them, soggy and none too pleased about it.

"At least we are back in the wholesome lands of Goldburg," said Reginald.

"I will be happy when we are back in the city," said Bijou, frowning, "And no sooner."

161

"Then let us be off," said her brother and led the way into the forest.

Fritz was about to follow when he heard a sudden fluttering of wings in the tree above him, and he looked up at the noise.

"Off where?" said something up there hidden in the dense branches of the tree.

"Hallo!" said the boy, "Who is that?"

Florian had stopped, too, and was trying to get a glimpse through the leaves, but he could see nothing. The unseen creature hopped from branch to branch, slowly descending, shaking and rustling the leaves as he went. Now even the Dumonts took notice as the creature spoke again:

"I am up here."

"Yes, but what is your name up there?" said Fritz, "Tell me that, and I may answer your question."

"Those who know me call me Hobs," said the creature, "And since you now know me, you may call me that."

"But I don't know you," said Fritz, and that was the truth because the creature was still hidden, "I cannot see you."

Another fluttering of wings came from the trees and a swishing of leaves and branches as they were pushed aside. Suddenly, out popped the large shape of a full-grown barn owl. He flapped clumsily this way and that, and flopped and fell down to the forest floor. He stood with his head cocked to one side and examined the four of them.

"Now, tell me, where are you off to?"

"A rather inquisitive creature, aren't you?" said Reginald, shaking his head, "What business is it of yours where we are off to? Fly along, owl, and let us be gone."

"*Woot, woot,*" said Hobs, puffing himself up and shaking his feathers, "I meant no harm. Only you come blundering through my territory, scaring off my easily-had dinner of mice and muskrats near the river. I think I have a right to know what you are about!"

Fritz, as always, tried to be the polite voice of the group.

"We are just passing through to the West. To Goldburg, that is."

"Goldburgers, huh?" said Hobs, narrowing his eyes at them.

"No, only those two are," said Florian.

"They are our guides," said Fritz.

"Yes, and we should like to continue guiding," said Bijou, "If you don't mind."

"*Woot, woot,* I don't mind," said Hobs, his feathers still quite puffed up, "But let me ask you this. May I accompany you? I have business that way anyhow, and it would be nice to have companions."

Before the Dumonts could speak, Fritz exclaimed, "Of course you can! We would be happy to have one more. And I have always heard that owls were very wise creatures."

"Oh, well now, *woot, woot*," said Hobs, wiggling in humble embarrassment, "I do not know how wise I am. But perhaps...compared to some..."

Reginald struck a match and puffed at his pipe, but the water of the Rushing River had dampened the tobacco so much that the flame sizzled out as soon as it touched the packing.

"Blasted thing," said the small man, "Can we just be off already?"

"All right," said Fritz with a smile.

So the group marched on, their numbers one greater, and perhaps very much wiser for that.

Hobs the barn owl proved very learned in the ways of the dark forest, and this was a very good thing. For the deeper they went underneath the trees, the darker it became. The canopy was so thick in places that the forest became almost as black as midnight, though the sun still shone in the sky beyond. Occasionally Reginald or Bijou tried to lead them one way, because it was lighter over there, but Hobs insisted they follow him through the darkest parts of the forest. The owl clearly knew best, however, because they never became lost and they kept a good pace, despite the tangles of the wood and the darkness.

Sometimes the right path leads through the most dismal of places.

Soon the sun dipped very low to the West, though it really made not one bit of difference in the shadowed wood. Yet now the dark took on a different character. It was no longer the dark of a shaded forest; now it was the dark of night.

Strange calls sounded in the distance, the cries and howls of night beasts. If not for the expert guidance of the owl, Fritz felt sure the Dumonts would have gotten them lost — or worse — in this dense forest.

The forest was not at all like the wild wood back home, and Fritz knew somehow this place was infinitely more ancient. A heavy stillness seemed to block the world without, and the trees stretched on so far that after a while one forgot there even *was* a world outside. The young boy had the feeling, too, from time to time that eyes watched him from the darkness, but he never saw anything and he did not mention this to the others.

Hobs seemed undaunted by any of these concerns; in fact, he was literally at home in this forest. Sometimes he waddled on his little owlish legs in front of the group, and sometimes he beat his great wings and soared far ahead of them. Once or twice, with a sudden *woot, woot,* the owl zoomed away into the shadows, only to return with the thin tail of a mouse or some other rodent peeking out of his sharp beak. Yet, he always came back to them, and he seemed happy to have friends.

Reginald and Bijou Dumont trudged on in growing displeasure. Bijou complained that had it not been for the others weighing her down, she could have flown all the way to Goldburg on her own. Reginald, on the other hand, grieved over the soggy loss of his pipe tobacco and cursed the Rushing River. Together the siblings made rather unpleasant traveling companions.

Fritz and Florian were simply exhausted; the last sleep they'd had was in the cottage of the golden-haired shepherdess. Much had happened since then, and Fritz yawned as he thought of how sore his feet were. The fox, too, had to give himself a good shake from snout to tail a couple of times to stay awake. Yet neither complained, because they were doing just what they had set out to do, venturing far west into the Lands Beyond the Moon.

After many miles passed without incident, Hobs alighted on Fritz's shoulder and perched there to the young boy's surprise. The others took no notice, but walked on in silence. Hobs leaned close to the boy's ear and said:

"*Whoo, yoohoo…*You, my young friend, you and your fox seem to be the most level-headed of this expedition. And I would speak to the fox, but I think he would not like that too much. In the past, I have probably eaten some of his distant relatives—nothing personal, that is just my nature—anyway, I think it is best to speak to you about this."

"About what?" asked Fritz, glad the wise owl had chosen him in whom to confide.

"*Woo-w*-well, we are about to enter a wicked part of the forest," said Hobs, "A part that has been taken over by some rather dangerous gnomes."

"Gnomes? What are those?"

"Dreadful, disgusting little creatures," said Hobs, snapping off each syllable with an audible click of his sharp beak, "They dwell underground in a series of tunnels near here. And my business, I'm afraid, is with them."

"But if they are such dreadful creatures, what business could you have with them?"

"*Shoo, hoo*, shhh, be quiet, lad," said Hobs, looking nervously back and forth, "I do not want those others to hear. And yes, the gnomes are as dreadful as I said. Horrid little beasts that creep through reeking mud and wallow in the peat bogs. Believe me, I do not *want* any business with them. But I have it nonetheless. They stole something from me…and I mean to get it back."

"What did they steal?" said Fritz, making sure to keep his voice down this time.

"They stole something that does not belong to me, and so it is doubly important that I get it back," said Hobs.

"I don't understand."

"A long time ago, many years before the present troubles in the Vale, a young maiden of royal blood gave to me a precious gemstone, a brilliant ruby that she called the Flame of Truth. She bade me guard and protect this ruby—she made me pledge my life to this—until she returns for it. And so I have, always awaiting the day of her triumphant return, guarding it faithfully...until one of those foul gnomes snuck into my nest and stole it!"

"Oh, then you must get it back," said Fritz, wanting to shout but trying to stay quiet so the Dumonts would not hear. The young boy knew, as all boys learn at some time or another, just how very important a promise made to a beautiful maiden could be.

"You simply must."

"*Toohoo, hoo, hoo*...Too true," said Hobs, "Too right you are. I must, and I will. But I do not want to get it back, only to have it fall into the hands of those Goldburgers. I do not trust them. I have known Goldburgers before."

"But Reginald said that Goldburg was a town where honest men lay their heads, a burg of wonders."

"It's a wonder that any honest man can keep his head in Goldburg," snorted Hobs.

"What do you mean?"

"Only this," said Hobs, as he raised a single talon and pointed at Reginald and Bijou, "Those two are tricky, and I do not want a tricky sort of help in recovering this ruby. The Flame of Truth is too precious a thing. I will trust it to you, boy, and to your fox."

"But how can we go off to deal with the gnomes without the Dumonts noticing we're gone?"

"*Yoohoo*, you just leave that to me," said the owl with a wink.

Chapter 15

Hobs the owl knew the forest well enough to get anyone hopelessly lost in it, and that is just what he planned to do with Reginald and Bijou Dumont. He did not tell Fritz exactly how, because he needed instead to quickly explain to the boy just what to expect from the gnomes.

"I've only see their underground lair once, and it was as narrow and twisting as a rabbit's warren. You and the fox should be able to make your way into the tunnels. I think they open up wider the farther down one goes…"

As the boy walked with the owl perched on his shoulder, Hobs gave him a general idea of the gnomes' lair and where those creatures might be hiding the Flame of Truth.

"Just watch out for the Nasty Gnome named Nod," was the last piece of advice the owl gave Fritz, "He is King of the Bog, and a dangerous brute."

"I don't like the idea of being underground with such nasty creatures," said Florian a few minutes later as Fritz whispered bits of the plan to him.

"Neither do I," said Fritz, "But Hobs believes this to be very important. And I think this is another of those things that Hanna spoke of…about helping with tribulations here in the Vale."

"I hope you are right," said Florian, "Otherwise we will have crawled around in the mud for nothing but a shiny rock."

Yet something about the name—the Flame of Truth—told Fritz that this was no mere shiny rock. Then there was the royal maiden who had entrusted it to Hobs; who had she been, and why had she not returned yet? Fritz agreed with the owl and believed that it was important to retrieve the ruby from those gnomes.

Fritz and Florian had no idea when Hobs would distract the Dumonts so they could sneak off toward the gnomes' lair. The owl seemed to be waiting for something as the group walked along. He kept turning his head this way and that, as if searching through the trees for some sign. The boy and the fox were just as surprised as Reginald and Bijou when the owl suddenly squawked and hopped from branch to branch as if he were being murdered.

"*Screeee, screeee!*" cried the owl in an ear-splitting screech. "*Screeee, screeeee!*"

"By the moon!" shouted Bijou, covering her ears, "What is it, you stupid creature?"

"I say, you silly squawking screecher, what are you going on about?" shouted Reginald.

"*Screeee, screeee!*" shrieked Hobs, "Run, run! There! Look there! The gnomes are out! Gnomes and goblins are come to get us! Their lantern approaches!"

Fritz looked to where the owl pointed, and had the young boy not known that this was all a diversion, he would have been utterly scared out of his wits. There, in the distance, hung a shimmering light that looked just like a dangling lamp held by some unseen hand.

"*Screeee, screeee!*" went Hobs again, "Death with his ghost-light approaches! Flee for your lives!"

And with that the owl flew away in a flurry of whirring wings.

Reginald and Bijou lost no time in following after the owl, leaving Fritz and Florian behind as they ran desperately for their lives from the grim figure of Death and his eerie lamp. The boy and the fox, meanwhile, felt no fear in the strange flickering light, knowing that Hobs had planned the whole charade. They stayed in their place and watched the light dance up and down, but do nothing more than that.

In truth, that weird spirit-lantern was what men on this side of the moon call a will-o'-the-wisp, for off in that direction, there was a deep peat bog. Hobs had known this and had chosen this spot for his diversion. As Fritz and Florian walked on to begin their search for the gnomes' cave, they smelled the pungent odor of the bog. It wafted to them in a smelly breeze. The stronger the smell became, the closer the two travelers knew they were to the cave of the gnomes.

Soon, they saw a sign sticking up out of the moist ground, scrawled over with the most hideous writing that Fritz had ever seen. It looked like it had been carved by a blind and drunk man, using his feet. And it read:

"Go back the way you came, or you've only yourself to blame!"

"Not a very welcoming sort of folk, are they?" said Florian with a smirk.

Fritz returned the grin, and the two travelers ignored the sign and made for the mouth of the cave. The entrance was nothing more than a muddy pit, a large round hole in the ground, smelling of damp earth and worms and many rotten things. It was a putrid door to the innards of the land. The gnomes posted no guard. To Fritz this made sense; why post a guard to such a horrid place? Who would ever *want* to get in here?

"Who, indeed?" said the boy to himself, thinking that he did not much care for the idea of going into that pit, especially since he knew what creatures called it home.

Florian looked uncertain as well. He said nothing, but Fritz knew the fox well enough now to recognize the worry on his face.

"Maybe we ought to go back and find Hobs," whispered the boy, as a bubble of foul air burped up from beneath the lip of the pit. "Tell him we couldn't do it."

"Maybe so…" said the fox, backing away.

Then, Fritz remembered the sweetness of the shepherdess Hanna and thought also of the nameless royal maiden who had entrusted the ruby to Hobs. The boy suddenly felt ashamed that he had even considered backing out.

"No, no," he said, patting Florian on the shoulder, "We must go in."

"I know. I just wanted you to say it."

The boy marched resolutely forward, and his little feet made sucking and squelching noises in the mud. The fox, however, padded lightly over the damp ground. When they reached the lip of the cave mouth, they leaned over. Fritz held his nose and looked sick. The smell of the gnome lair was almost overpowering.

"Nothing to do now but go in," said Florian, as if the words themselves tasted bad in his mouth.

So they went into the pit. Gently, they lowered themselves over the edge, found a foothold in the mud, and dropped down. They were on a sort of spiraling ramp that led down to another smaller opening, a little hole no bigger than the entrance to a rabbit's burrow.

"We'll have to squeeze through that," said the boy, not at all liking the prospect of wriggling into the putrid tunnel.

"I think we ought to be as quiet as possible," said Florian, "No telling when we might meet the gnomes."

Fritz nodded. Without another word, he crawled headfirst into the darkness. The walls of the tunnel hugged his shoulders as he crept down the slanting ground. Florian followed, having a much easier time.

After a while, the walls widened and Fritz was able to go rather quickly on his hands and knees. The tunnel continued to slant down into the muddy underbelly of the forest. Then, the way twisted a couple of times and led to a flat area like a landing.

Here, Fritz was able to rise up on his knees, but his head was only half an inch from the ceiling. Florian had no trouble moving about now and walked as easily as if he were above ground. They had still seen no gnomes and for that at least, the boy and the fox were happy.

So they slogged on through the muddy tunnel. The floor dipped down even more and the grimy ceiling stayed where it was, so that Fritz could walk on his feet with his back only slightly stooped. He walked like this until they came to a place where the tunnel split.

"I think we should go right," said Fritz without giving it much thought. The Watcher's advice seemed just as appropriate here as in the mountains.

"Undoubtedly," said Florian, as he remembered what happened the one time they had gone left.

The tunnel's right path went on its soggy way, deeper and deeper into the ground, and the travelers thought how strange it was that they had not spied a single gnome.

"Are you sure that we are in the right place?" said the fox, but Fritz did not have to answer.

For the companions had just come through a sort of sagging doorway into a wide room a bit like a lord's hall, and every inch of the room was filled with gnomes. There were gnomes of every sort: fat gnomes, skinny gnomes, gnomes with scarred faces, gnomes with scarred lips, gnomes with scarred everythings; gnomes with two claw-like hands and gnomes with only one hand and gnomes with no hands at all and even one gnome with a wrinkly hand that grew from the side of his face; gnomes with teeth the size of daggers and gnomes with teeth as flat and black as a smith's anvil and gnomes with no teeth at all, just slobbery little empty mouths; gnomes that were colored ghostly gray and mustard yellow and vomit green and muddy brown and blood red and every other unpleasant color that one could name; gnomes that spit and gnomes that snorted and gnomes that drooled and gnomes that laughed their little gnomish heads off at some vulgar gnomish joke; gnomes that jumped and hooted and hollered and gnomes that slapped other gnomes around for looking at them wrong.

In short, it was a lot of gnomes.

Never had Fritz seen such a collection of disgusting creatures assembled for such nothingness, but then again, the young boy had lived on a farm his whole life and had not been exposed to congressional government. As Fritz and Florian watched from their hidden perch, the gnomes caroused and carried on, drinking offensively and gnawing at chunks of meat. Other than that, they did very little but roll in the grime.

A few gnomes grunted in their gnomish language, a tongue that sounded as if it were made up entirely of profanities. It is not worth attempting to recreate any bit of that language here; only imagine the most foul-mouthed person that you have ever had the displeasure to run across and take him on his worst day when he is at his angriest and most filthy, and there you have just a tiny idea of what the gnomes sounded like.

As Fritz looked out over this teeming sea of nastiness, he muttered, "How will we ever get past them?"

Florian shook his head. The horrid creatures packed the place. There was no way through the hall without the gnomes seeing them. The fox looked uncertainly at the young boy whose clothes were covered in the mud of the tunnel and whose face was smeared with dirt. He had an idea.

"Maybe we can just walk right through them."

"Are you crazy?" said Fritz, "They'll catch us!"

"Not if they think we are one of them," said Florian, squinting his eyes and sizing up the boy, "I think if you coat yourself with a little more filth, you just might be able to pass as a gnome. You're the right size anyway."

"Of course!" exclaimed the boy in an excited whisper. He picked up a handful of mud and daubed it on his skin. Then, he wiped some on the fox.

"And you, too! If we are disgusting enough, we can hide in plain sight."

So the two of them set to rolling about in the yuck and the muck, slathering themselves with thick globs of mud. After a few minutes of wallowing like pigs, the two were coated in a goopy layer of sludge and grime. Not an inch of them was left clean, but every bit covered in a gooey mess.

Fritz smiled and his teeth gleamed like pearls in a bog. He said with the utter delight that only a young boy can muster in such a condition:

"We're repulsive!"

"Yes, but now we must act the part," said Florian.

Fritz nodded and hunched his back and twisted his neck to one side and let out an animalistic grunt.

"How's this?" said the boy and took a few steps, dragging one leg and snarling like he'd tasted something foul.

"Sickening," said the fox and added, "It's perfect."

Florian affected his own gnomish walk, and the two boldly went toward the crowd of cruel creatures in the hall. The companions were about to find out just how convincing they were as gnomes.

Chapter 16

The disguises worked perfectly.

None of the gnomes gave them a second look as the two travelers pushed their way through the packed hall. Most of the creatures were preoccupied with their own filthy activities, whether that was tearing the legs off a rabbit and chomping on them raw, or having a contest to see who could blow the biggest snot bubble. A time or two, Fritz saw something that made him want to vomit, but even if he had vomited, the boy probably would have just fit in all the better.

The whole scene was the most frightfully nasty place that the boy had ever imagined. If a pile of sewage could be suddenly brought to life, then it would not look very much different from these gnomes.

Luckily none of the creatures seemed suspicious of intruders in their midst. Fritz and Florian walked on rather easily, or as easily as one can in a underground chamber full of gnomes. The two pushed and shoved and jostled their way through the crowds, but no one noticed anything odd. This was how gnomes moved about as a rule; they are rather rude and impolite to each other just as much as to others.

On and on, the two companions walked, and yet on and on continued the crowds of gnomes. Finally the boy and the fox pushed their way to the end of the hall. At this far end, off to the right, was a short corridor that spiraled down into the gloom. Fritz and Florian made for this entrance, but they found it guarded by two chubby gnomes that looked a little like twins. Both were short and had great rolls of fat around their midsection that looked like waves of grayish flesh.

One of the guards grumbled something in Gnomish at the two companions. Fritz did not understand the language, but somehow he felt that he should be insulted. When neither he nor Florian replied, the other guard grunted something else.

This sounded worse.

Fritz knew he had to say something or their cover would be blown. He opened his mouth and realized that he was about to be polite, as one usually is when meeting strangers. That would not be at all right down here; he had to be as unpleasant as possible.

"Get out of the way, you moron!" said Fritz, "We've come to see King Nod."

"*Pfft!*" spit the first guard, "He don't even speak proper Gnomish an' he wanta see the King o' the Bog."

"*Achh!*" hacked the second guard, "Ye must be a surface dweller, ain't ye? Ye smell like the sun. And a bit like fresh air. I can't abide fresh air."

"Are you going to let us see the Nasty Gnome or not?" said Florian, being as mean as he could be, "We have business with him. And I bet he would like to tear the heads off two stupid guards who held up the Bog King's business."

"*Ughuh!*" coughed the first guard, while the second looked on in terror, "I seen him do that very same thing to my pred—my, uh, predecess—my, oh the guy who was guard before me!"

"Aye, ye must be the servers. Pass on then, ye," said the second guard, motioning into the corridor with a wicked-looking axe blade, "Git down there, and we'll see iffen the Bog King don't but bite the heads off ye, too."

When the two companions had walked on down the corridor and were out of earshot of the gnome guards, Fritz said, "It worked!"

"Yes, but I hope we don't actually meet King Nod down here," said Florian, "And that no heads are bitten off."

Fritz knew that the ruby called the Flame of Truth was probably somewhere near the Bog King, but the boy hoped that there would be some way to steal the gem without coming face to face with the Nasty Gnome himself.

Down the tunnel, they came to what must have been the door to the throne room of the King of the Bog. Its arched frame was decorated and outlined with the bones of every animal imaginable, and Fritz thought he saw a bone or two that belonged to humans. The keystone of the arch was made from the very large skull of what must have been an enormous horse; Fritz was immediately reminded of the Council of Wild Horses and wondered if this horse had been a relative of the great silver stallion.

Fritz and Florian passed quietly under the skull and into the throne room. There were no other gnomes present, but they felt no great relief, for Nod, the King of the Bog himself, sat on his massive throne at the end of the hall. The throne was made of more bones and the spaces between these bones were packed solid with mud and manure. The hall smelled of every wretched and miserable scent imaginable, but the only sound was a rumbling from deep within the king's phlegm-y chest.

The king was snoring.

His bulky body leaned to one side, and he slept up there on his great chair. As his head lulled and rolled to one side, his broad forehead gleamed with a bright light, and Fritz saw that the light came from a brilliant ruby. King Nod wore the Flame of Truth in the crown on his fat head.

"Oh, no," whispered Florian when he saw the same thing.

"At least he is asleep," said Fritz, "We'll just have to sneak up and take it."

But that plan quickly fell apart, because just as Fritz and Florian took another step into the throne room, the great Bog King stirred on his seat. He grunted and grumbled and raised his massive head, and then after hacking and retching a bit, he said:

"Who comes into my magnificent presence?"

Fritz and Florian froze in fear, certain that they would be killed by the creature. When they said nothing, King Nod said:

"*Ach*, it's about time you two got here. I am starved. Fetch me meat and drink from my chambers. Hurry now, or I will eat you."

Without hesitation, the two companions followed his orders. They played along and went to where the sausage-like finger of the king pointed. This led them into a pantry of sorts, little more than a makeshift room dug out of the mud.

There they found a heaping plate piled high with decomposing rodents of all kinds and festering fish and rotten mushrooms and overripe pomegranates, and all of this sprinkled very liberally with crickets and spiders. Beside this was a tall chalice, a cup filled to the brim with swamp water. On the floor at the back of the pantry, however, were three large barrels of beer that had been cracked open at the top and smelled as if they had gone bad. Fritz stared at these and an idea came to him.

He took the king's cup, dumped out the swamp water, and filled it up with the skunky beer. The dark brown liquid sloshed in the cup as he walked it back to the king. Florian walked beside him, bearing the plate of food on the top of his foxy head. The two bowed in front of His Muddy Majesty, and King Nod took the plate and cup and fell to eating and drinking in a gnomish fashion.

At the first taste of the stale and skunky beer, the Bog King let fly a few obscenities and then added, "That's no swamp water! The buggers always bring me swamp water! But this beer is a mighty treat!"

The huge creature downed the rest of the cup in one great gulp. The ruby on his crown flashed fiercely as he tossed his head back to burp.

"Can I get you some more?" said Fritz, catching the cup as the Nasty Gnome dropped it.

"More?" said the king, "The fools never think to offer more! That's why I kill so many of them. Of course I would like more!"

Fritz ran off to the pantry to fetch another cup of the rotten drink. Florian seemed to have caught on to the plan. He concealed a smile as Fritz brought back another cup of skunky beer. King Nod drained this cup just as quickly. Then another went down, and then another.

The king drank the beer as fast as the boy could run to the pantry to fetch it. On one trip to the pantry, Fritz found a couple of old wooden bowls and filled these with beer, too. When he was before the king and the gnome finished drinking the cup, the boy immediately offered up a bowl.

The Nasty Gnome chuckled with delight, fell to coughing up some phlegm, and then chuckled with more delight. He snatched up the bowl and downed the beer with slobbery slurps.

"More?" said Fritz, the second bowl ready.

"Oh, ho! Much and more!" cried King Nod, "Keep it coming!"

Spider legs and the tail of a lizard hung out of the king's mouth as he munched and drank at the same time. Cup after cup, bowl after bowl, Fritz ran to the king and the skunky brew went down his throat one after another, until Florian, who had been watching with laughing eyes, lost count.

When the second barrel was completely drained and Fritz had just started on the third, the King of the Bog began to drowse. He was very drunk indeed, and it was a good thing that he was sitting down. His huge frame would have made quite a dent in the mud if he collapsed on the floor. He burped and the whole room filled with the brownish stench of beer. Then, his head fell forward on his broad chest and the lights went out in his eyes. Fritz's plan had worked. The Nasty Gnome had passed out.

"Quick," whispered the boy, "We must get the ruby before he wakes up."

Yet even standing on his tiptoes, Fritz could not reach the gemstone. The gnome was too tall and the chair he sat on too high.

"Let me help you," said Florian, crouching down, "Stand on my back."

Fritz would never have been able to get the stone without his friend. The fox gave him a lift, just high enough to grab the edge of the high seat. The boy pulled himself up, and making sure not to rouse the king, he climbed as carefully as possible up to the king's head. The drunken breath that whistled out of the gnome's lips made Fritz's stomach turn, but the boy focused on his task. Reaching out, he pried at the red stone with all his might and suddenly — *POP!* — out came the ruby.

Fritz fell backward and tumbled into the mud, clutching the precious Flame of Truth.

"You did it," said Florian with excitement, "Now all we have to do is sneak back through the outer hall."

But this excitement was short-lived, and the chance for sneaking lost, because at that very same moment, the two guards from earlier appeared in the entrance to the throne room.

"*Argh!* He's stealing the red rock!" yelled one guard.

"Ye sorry surface dweller! I'll kill ye!" yelled the other.

Fritz slipped the ruby into his knapsack and held it tight.

"O Nasty Gnome, wake up, King o' the Bog!" the guards cried, but the drunken king did not stir. Yet the cries and shrieks of the gnomes were heard up in the outer hall, and that horde of creatures came running at once toward the throne room.

Fritz and Florian were trapped.

As the writhing hordes of gnomes pushed forward like a tide of deadly water, Fritz and Florian looked desperately for some means of escape. But there was only one door in or out of this throne room, and that was blocked by gnomes intent on killing them. Behind the pair, the huge slobbering mass of drunkenness that was King Nod titled sideways as he leaned against the arm of the throne.

A particularly gnarly-looking gnome reached out and grabbed Fritz's arm and yanked the boy forward into the swarm. If not for the quick action of the fox, Fritz would have been completely overwhelmed. But Florian leapt forward, his teeth flashing as he bit the gnome's arm. The creature screamed and let go.

It was then that Fritz remembered Father's sharp dagger. He had worn the dagger on his belt since he left his parents' farm and yet he'd had no cause to use it. Now he drew the dagger and waved it in front of him, holding off the gnomes.

"Ye can't fight us all!" spit a gnome.

"He's right," said Florian, growling, "We've got to do something."

Fritz saw only one way to go, and that was backward.

"Up on the throne!" he said to the fox, "Climb!"

This would buy them a little time at least, even if they were ultimately overrun by the vicious gnomes. Fritz began to despair that he and Florian would be torn apart by these horrid creatures. There were just too many of them; every gnome underground seemed to have packed into the throne room. Fritz clung desperately to the dagger as he climbed the throne.

When the gnomes followed them, the boy and the fox scrambled up the king's body until they perched on top of his head. The poking and prodding and shoving soon awoke the drunken king, and the huge gnome suddenly pitched forward. Only by great luck and a firm grip did Fritz and Florian manage to cling to his crown.

As the King of the Bog stirred, his trunk-like arms hurled the littler gnomes off the throne. With lumbering movements, the king rose slowly and unsteadily to his feet. The giant gnome swayed this way and that, like a top that is coming to the end of a long spin.

The crowds of gnomes backed away in terror from their fearsome leader. Even having such a good reason as attacking intruders did not give those lesser gnomes the right to approach their king. They cowered back, lowering their eyes and bowing in respect to the Nasty Gnome Nod, who looked around the throne room uncertainly. For a moment, Fritz and Florian were forgotten by the crowd.

But only for a moment.

Then, Nod bellowed in a deep, rumbling voice and yelled at the two travelers, "I will kill you and crush you and crunch your bones!"

Yet the Bog King was still very drunk, and he stumbled around the throne room, crushing instead his underlings, crunching the littler gnomes underneath his great feet. Nod sent others flying violently into the wall as he swung his immense arms wildly. As Nod reached for the two travelers on his head, Fritz suddenly jabbed the sharp dagger into the gnome's fat neck.

The Nasty Gnome roared in pain. The excitement of the fight and the generous meal and large portions of old beer all mixed to produce a rather revolting result: Nod, the King of the Bog, retched all over the crowd of gnome subjects. The wave swamped the littler gnomes, and then to add to this, their giant king pitched forward and fell with a mighty crash. The drunken gnome had passed out again, his head splashing into the mud right near the doorway.

This was a bit of good luck for Fritz and Florian, who rolled right out into the hallway, the mass of angry creatures behind them. Many gnomes had been killed by their own king, and the living ones were sloshing their way through the nastiness to give chase.

Fritz and Florian wasted no time. The boy clutched the ruby called the Flame of Truth, and the two travelers ran for their lives out of the gnome tunnels.

Chapter 17

In no time at all, Fritz and Florian ran back through the outer hall and up into the smaller tunnels near the surface. All the while, behind them they could hear the squishing and plopping of many gnome feet running through the mud. Worse than this was the sound of the language that the gnomes shrieked at the two as they fled. There are no words in the languages of Men to even come close to the hatred and filth that these creatures spewed that day.

Fritz wiggled through the narrow opening and could see the great pit ahead. Florian followed close behind, and soon the two squirmed from the tunnel into the open air again. The first breath of semi-fresh air filled their lungs like a refreshing drink on a hot day. Yet the horrid stench of the bog still filled the place, and now the two had to clamber out of the pit.

The fox jumped out of it easily enough, but the boy's feet still dangled over the edge when the gnomes swarmed out like ants from an anthill.

Claws tore at the boy's ankles, but Florian tugged at his clothes with his teeth and pulled Fritz to safety.

Back on solid ground, the two travelers broke into a run through the forest, fleeing from the angry bog creatures. Fritz and Florian had to reunite with Hobs and the Dumonts, but they had no idea where those three had gone after the owl's distraction. Neither had the horde of gnomes slackened in their deadly rage now that they were above ground. Fritz could not remember a time when he had ever run so fast, and always the fox stayed ahead of him. Both knew that if they slowed at all, they would be ripped to pieces by hundreds of wrathful gnomes.

Under branches and over roots and between the trunks of trees, they ran on, dipping, ducking, and dodging their way through the forest. They headed as west as they could reckon. The shrieks and cries of the charging gnomes spread until the whole forest echoed with their filth.

After long, exhausting minutes of running, Fritz and Florian began to hear another sound. The familiar *woot, woot* of a certain owl sounded from somewhere in the distance. The two companions headed toward this sound, and much to their surprise, they soon fell in right next to Hobs and the Dumont siblings.

Reginald and Bijou Dumont ran for their lives in front of the gnome swarm as well, and Hobs the owl flew smoothly and gracefully under the twisted trees. The group was back together, but no safer for that.

"Run!" said Fritz, but he need not have said anything at all.

The haggard group ran and ran, until Fritz thought that his legs would surely give out and he would fall to the creatures of the bog. As he fled west, the air around him freshened, but still echoed with the wicked cries of the gnomes.

"How…will…we…ever…make…it…" panted Fritz as he ran.

The boy was right to be worried, and if he had ever seen a victim of a gnome attack before, he would have been downright panicked. At least they seemed to be nearing the edge of the forest. The tangled undergrowth grew thicker as the trees all around grew shorter and shorter. Yet no change in environment was going to save them from the charging gnomes.

Instead, they were saved by something altogether unexpected.

The sudden blast of a war horn heralded their rescue. And the pounding feet of a score of horses played harmony with the sweet lowing of the horn. Fritz looked for the source of this beautiful thundering music and saw a group of twenty riders bearing down from the north. Their sharp lance heads aimed straight for the mass of gnomes, and the collision was dreadful.

Fritz could not watch. He'd had enough of battle for a lifetime. All he knew was that they had been saved by these mystery riders. The cursing gnomes, the ones who had survived the initial charge, fled back into the forest, back to the bog and their smelly pit.

Fritz collapsed in the dirt at the edge of the forest, his body utterly spent. The last thing he remembered was the sight of the mounted men standing over him, looking down through the visors of their helms.

When the boy awoke, he sat in a saddle, the slow stride of a horse rocking him back and forth with the gentleness of a mother rocking her child. He was not alone in the saddle, but sat in front of a knight who held the reins. Blinking and gazing all around in wonder, Fritz saw the other members of his group riding the same way in other saddles. Even Hobs the owl had his leg tied to a saddle horn so that he could not fly away. Fritz worried that they had escaped the gnomes only to fall into a worse fate.

His worries were dispelled when he heard Reginald Dumont speaking with one of the riders.

"I say, my good Goldburger," spoke the small gentleman, not very cheerfully, "Listen here, do you know who I am?"

"I know you are coming to Goldburg with us," said the rider in a disinterested voice, "I care little for ought else. The lord of the city will know what to do with you."

"See here, you! I can tell you right now what to do with us," said Reginald, shaking his finger at the man, "Skip the lord. Take us straight to the Queen! To the Castle in the Sky! She will want to see us."

"The Queen," snorted another rider, "Why would Her Majesty want to see you?"

"I will tell you, if you will just listen, you fool! I am Reginald Dumont, and she there is my sister, Bijou! Maybe you know those names, huh?"

The riders slowed their horses, and the looks on their faces told clearly that they did, in fact, recognize the names.

"Your pardons, sir," said one of the Goldburg riders as he quickly unbound Reginald's hands.

Fritz wondered at this abrupt change. The Dumonts must be important people, indeed. Now at least the traveling group was safe. The two animals were likewise released, and Fritz's own hands were untied, too. The boy breathed a sigh of relief to be in the company of such an armed escort. And that was not even the best thing of all, because Reginald said:

"Now that you have come to your senses, my men, I want you to take us to the Queen of the Castle in the Sky. I bring good tidings to her!"

"Of course," said the leader of the riders.

Fritz's heart leapt inside of him. The Queen! He was not only safe, but now he was bound to see a queen. What a sudden turnaround in their fortunes, in such a short time to go from the Bog King's lair to the Castle in the Sky.

The rest of the journey to Goldburg passed in sleepy silence, as Fritz and his tired companions dozed on and off in the saddle. Soon the boy saw the reason for the city's name as the whole group passed under the gleaming golden gates of Goldburg.

The rest of the golden city was a great wonder as well, but how many great wonders have been forgotten by travel-weary boys who could not keep their eyes open? Such was the case with Fritz on that golden dawn. Although the sun shone over the Vale, Fritz's eyes drooped heavily and he remembered little of his entrance into Goldburg.

The whole group slept in the lord's manor house, a sprawling walled estate in the middle of the city. They slept for long, restful hours, all day and night and into the next morning. The high gold wall blocked out most of the city noise, and outside the window of Fritz's room, there was the additional buffer of a back garden with its well-groomed hedgerows and ancient trees. The whispering leaves of fall laid their death-golden blanket on the garden floor, and on the street beyond the garden wall. This covering, dampened by a mist that lay heavy on the city that morning, muffled the footsteps of servants coming and going, and the flow of traffic beyond the estate passed with only the quiet squish of soggy leaves.

When Fritz awoke, it was midday, and every second of sleep had taken the weariness from his body like a roaring fire takes the moisture from wet clothing. Sometime in the night he had bathed, or been bathed, because all the grime of the gnome-caves had been washed away. He stood by the window and looked out at the Goldburg lord's garden and breathed deeply that gratifying scent of a dying year and all its golden autumnal wonders.

Yet he felt nothing like he had when he and Florian awoke in the cottage of the golden-haired shepherdess Hanna. He was well-rested certainly, but felt none of the immense joy as he had on that far-off morning. Here, instead, the waking brought an aching expectation and not a little apprehension. He was anxious to meet the Queen of the Castle in the Sky.

When Fritz had dressed, he ran out into the garden to find the rest of the group ready to set off again. Fritz whispered to Hobs and secretly offered to give him the Flame of Truth, but the owl shook his head fiercely.

"Keep it secret," he said, "And keep it close to your heart."

The boy nodded and kept the ruby hidden securely in an inner pocket of his wolf's skin coat.

The lord of Goldburg met them in the garden, too, a tall, tubby and mustachioed man with great, shivering jowls that reminded Fritz of a smaller, human version of Nod. This fat lord shook Fritz's hand vigorously, but there was no friendliness in the greeting as one would expect from a gracious host; there was only the formality of an older gentleman and politician who knew that it was expected of a man of his station to shake the hands of small children and smile at them. But Fritz found the smile as discomforting as the smell of the gnome pits. It made the man's face look even uglier, and did nothing to improve the boy's first impression of the lord of Goldburg.

No doubt he was a well-liked lord in his city, but Fritz found his attempts at charm fell utterly flat. Many of the big man's jokes that brought roaring laughter from Reginald or Bijou, only made Fritz frown and shake his head. There was something at work in this that has happened just as often on this side of the moon; Fritz, sweet innocent Fritz, saw the lord of Goldburg as he really was: ugly and rude and rather a phony fellow. The boy was ignorant or at least unmoved by the unspoken adult agreement that tends to give such men of office an air of power and irreproachability. He only knew that he didn't like him.

Fritz felt eager to be off all the more now that he had met the owner of this estate. The Castle in the Sky awaited them, and one could not linger on the ground. The boy was happy when finally he walked with Hobs perched on his shoulder out of the estate's gate, accompanied by Reginald and Bijou, and of course, good old Florian the fox.

The Dumonts led the way through the city, which for all purposes looked much like a twin to Whitlee. The only difference was that here, despite the many gilded buildings that glittered and shined, this golden city seemed darker somehow. Everything seemed to have a shadow cast over it, even at the peak of midday, so that the gold trim and gold statues seemed tarnished; of course, gold does not tarnish, so Fritz could not see how this could be.

Even high on the ramparts of the western wall where the group now walked, a peculiar dimness clung to the city. It was almost like some persistent sickness in the brick and mortar itself, like that last straggling cough that lingers long after the cold proper has run its course. Fritz did not understand it. The people within could be, but how could a city be sick? Buildings and walls were made of wood and stone and glass, and these had no feelings. Did they?

How could the very stones cry out?

Fritz did not give it too much thought, but turned his mind back to the West, deeper into the

Lands Beyond the Moon. There, far away yet, another swelling line of hills and mountains reared up, higher than any he imagined could ever exist. So high were these craggy mountains that no summits could be seen from where he stood. Perhaps there were no summits at all, only rising mountains, rising, ever rising. Fritz could not conceive of anything beyond such mountains, and began to wonder if those mountains were, after all, the End of Everything.

Then, the boy looked to the sky, that wide endless firmament that whispered promises of hidden castles amidst its drifting cloudbanks. He squinted so to see as far into the pale distance as he could, but all he saw up there, soaring in spacious circles on an updraft, was the black shape of a hawk or eagle or some other great bird of prey.

"How will we reach the Queen?" he asked, "Is there a stair to the Castle in the Sky?"

"A stair!" exclaimed Reginald, patting the boy's shoulder as an adult will do when he thinks a child's words are ridiculous, "No, my boy, no such stair was ever built to reach the sky's secret splendors."

"But how..."

"The only way up is to fly," said Reginald.

"But Florian and I cannot fly," said Fritz.

"Yes, you are an inconvenience, aren't you?" said Bijou, who had not been at all friendly since being freed from prison. She pulled the black raven's feather from her robe again and twirled it in the boy's face.

"I guess I'll have to carry you up, won't I?" she said, as her arms sprouted into coal-colored wings as easily as a normal person would slip on a coat.

"Well, don't just stand there, boy, grab hold."

So he did, and Florian as well, and Reginald. Bijou lifted off from the wall with her whirring black wings. Hobs needed no help to follow alongside as they soared higher and higher. Once, Fritz looked down and saw the city of Goldburg falling away until it seemed no more than a gold spot on a map.

But enough with looking behind!

The boy lifted his eyes, as the cloudbanks parted like the salt sea against the prow of a ship, and there he saw a sight that never left his memory for all the long years after.

The Castle in the Sky floated in the blue yonder.

Chapter 18

As an island appears to a sailor in the featureless sea, so did that hovering land appear out of the bluish haze. The Castle in the Sky perched upon the nothingness, with only the empty air beneath, as if a great mountain had been suddenly scooped up by some unseen hand and hung dangling on a line.

As lightly as a cloud, the expanse of land floated in the sky. Much of it was dominated by the castle itself, but there lay also the sprawl of its city, and outside of those huge walls, rolled lush fields of wheat and barley enclosed by neat hedgerows and narrow country lanes. The farmland stretched out like a flourishing carpet in front of the castle. In these fields could be seen scores of laborers working to bring in the last of the harvest.

Scythes swung through the air with a rhythmic swish and the familiar conversations of harvesters drifted to Fritz's ears as Bijou flew closer. The men and women in the fields were not unlike the men and women in the fields back home around his parents' farm. How was it that there should be such likeness between places so ordinary and the Lands Beyond the Moon? How a resemblance between the everyday and the otherworldly? Here was a floating castle, home to a queen of enchantments, and her subjects were engaged in such ordinary banter.

Fritz realized that he had never expected such simplicity to coexist so easily with the fantastic. The boy began to wonder if perhaps there was, in fact, just as much of the fantastic back in the lands around home, in the fields he knew. Perhaps beside the commonplace so dominant there were hidden bits and pieces of the fantastic, just as here the fantastic dominated but revealed hints of the ordinary.

There would be plenty of time to think on this later. Just then, Bijou was flying them over these harvest fields, and the men and women waved as they soared overhead. The castle and its city drew closer, and the skyline filled Fritz's vision.

The city revealed her countless spires, soaring belfry towers, columns, obelisks, and massive cathedral-like buildings with flying buttresses, all amidst a sea of domes crowned by richly ornamented cupolas. Fritz had heard of the glories of Rome and Constantinople, but here was a Byzantine dream that surpassed even the wildest imaginations of those distant emperors.

When the parsons and friars had spoken of a New Jerusalem and all its glories, the boy had not understood. Now Fritz thought they might have been thinking of a place like this.

In that moment, the architecture of the grand city seemed to give stone-shape to the longing in his soul. Fritz saw before him what he had always felt within. Here in this place was the emotion made physical; some master craftsman had turned yearning into walls, caught emotion in the mortar and raised a monument to the hopeful horizon. How like a shadow seemed the lands of Earth now! What dim reflection of beauty was behind him, now thrown into vast relief by this city.

And yet Fritz knew in his heart that this place was not the source of the Light anymore than the moon was. This Castle in the Sky and its city were only reflections themselves. He knew this because they offered no satisfaction, no relief. They did not quench the thirst or quell the hunger, but only intensified them. The pangs inside the boy only grew in the presence of the city, as you grow hungrier when you smell intensely the scent of freshly baked bread or sizzling bacon. Only eating will help, but here in this city was but the fragrance and not the food.

All of this came to the young boy in silence, and he spoke not a word of it to the others as they flew closer. He did catch Florian's eye at one moment, and he thought that perhaps the fox understood what he felt.

Bijou set them down just outside of the front gate of the city. Now that their group was on level ground, the walls stood even more enormous before them. Fritz had to crane his neck all the way back just to see the ramparts. The gate was a solid marble arch carved with reliefs all over, and in hollows around it, were gilded statues of heroes or saints that must have won honor sometime long ago.

"Are we going to see the Queen right away?" said Fritz, marveling at the impressive entrance.

"Why do you think I brought you here?" said Bijou, as she strode purposefully forward. A few black feathers drifted in her wake.

"Come, come, my boy," said Reginald, trotting alongside his sister.

"Let us be careful," whispered Florian, ever the voice of reason.

Fritz patted his friend on his red-orange back and whispered, "Of course."

Hobs alighted on Fritz's shoulder, and nipped playfully at the boy's ear, as the three of them followed the Dumonts into the city. Inside, the people who lived in the sky watched the ground dwellers as you would watch circus folk who suddenly came tramping into your town. A few of the young children waved and shouted happily at Fritz, who smiled and returned their greeting.

A make-shift parade seemed to have been gotten up, and the sidewalks soon filled and the streets became lined with spectators watching the Dumonts and their companions. A general murmur went amongst the crowd that here was an emissary come to meet the Queen, an envoy that had come from far away to speak with Her Majesty.

"What a welcome!" said Fritz, who was not used to such attention.

The boy wondered just what he had gotten himself into by crossing the Milky Way and the Mountains of the Moon. These people all watched him with expectant faces, and they clearly believed that he had come to them for some reason. He only hoped that he could live up to their expectations, whatever they turned out to be.

The walk up the well-maintained streets passed quickly enough, though the city was large. Soon their group neared the Castle in the Sky itself, that massive fortress-palace that was the seat of rule over the Vale of Abundance. Imagine all the castles that you have ever seen in your life, then throw that out, because the Castle in the Sky was like none of those.

Fritz had never imagined that such a place could exist, such striking combination of beauty and power, a building fit for a warrior-queen. The loveliness of its gilded exterior was surpassed only by the domination of its imposing curtain wall and its turrets. The portcullis was fashioned from many-colored steel. The arrowslits had stained glass windows in them, which undoubtedly were removed in the event the loop holes were ever needed for battle. Beyond these fanciful outer defenses were other signs of military might: stables full of trained warhorses of all kinds—destriers, coursers and rounceys; catapults ready for firing, large enough to lob missiles over the wall; and armories that were filled with swords and pikes and spears and maces and mauls and morning stars and war hammers.

All this could be seen through the wide open gate, and through another set of arches off to the left in what was apparently a yard dedicated solely to the military. When Fritz looked straight ahead, however, he saw a long, broad aisle that led into the castle. The group followed this path with its magnificent granite arches that lined the building façades on either side, and shortly they passed through an inner wall.

Here a beautifully sculpted marble man, dressed in white robes smooth as silk, flowing as if caught by a heavy wind and yet unmoving, stood in a courtyard garden surrounded by abundant flowers and lush hanging plants. The sculpture wore the expression of a warrior, and his broad chest and powerful arms rippled with marble muscles, as his great hand clutched a sword of stone. Frozen thus, he held eternal watch over the entrance to the glories beyond.

Yet it was clear from the first glance that the statue sentinel was missing something, though what that was the boy could not exactly say. In the hilt of his sword, an empty space showed, a hollow of some sort that seemed as if it should have been filled by something. And so the marble man, handsome though he was, looked rather incomplete, as if the artist had forgotten some last finishing touch.

Fritz could not quite put his finger on this aspect of the statue — only later would he realize there had been a hollow space in the sword — but he knew something was not right. Yet Reginald seemed to find the entire statue utterly hideous, turning up his nose at it, and Bijou even spit on the marble man's feet as they passed. Why those two should want to treat such a beautiful statue so poorly was outside of Fritz's understanding.

Hobs leaned in close to the boy's ear and said, "*Woohoo-woo, what* rude and boorish folk!"

Florian overheard and nodded.

Yet Fritz's attention had already been drawn to the staircase ahead, hundreds of stairs that led to the entrance to the Queen's hall. Some artist had made each step into a mosaic depicting scenes from the long storied history of the Lands Beyond the Moon. Of course, the young boy did not recognize any of the scenes, but the overall effect struck him as remarkable.

As they climbed these steps to enter the hall, Fritz remembered that solitary march he had once made through the Mountains of the Moon when he had struck up a fine tune and swung his knapsack on a makeshift lance above his head. He was still no knight, but he tried to portray a knightly character. He stood as tall and straight as possible, and kept his chin high, and his chest swelled out, even though the heart within it thumped wildly with nervousness.

The great doors of the hall flung open by some unknown force, and the travelers strode in. Hobs, for some reason, lingered outside, flying off to perch on a rooftop without a word. Fritz shrugged and let the owl go.

The boy had no idea what to expect of the Queen of the Castle in the Sky. She must be quite a woman to live in a place so fantastic, but he wondered what she would look like. He realized that he had been picturing in his mind an elderly matron deep in wisdom and weighed down with long years of rule.

The boy was surprised then to find the Queen so young. She was a maiden of an age with that golden-haired shepherdess he and Florian had met so far away. This young Queen sat on her throne at the far end of the hall, dressed in gold-trimmed finery, and the room dwarfed her small frame. Where Hanna had been fair-haired, the Queen had locks of the deepest black, as beautiful as lustrous onyx and as shiny. Where that other maiden had exuded warmth, this beautiful queen seemed to drawn in all the warmth of the room and give forth only a glowing coldness.

She was no less an attractive creature, only different, and Fritz found himself captivated by this crowned maiden and her cool and silvery eyes. She wore a gray floor-length dress accented by cloth-of-gold, cinched tightly at the waist by a silken belt that held a bouquet of flowers in its knot. Around her shapely neck were many dazzling pieces of jewelry.

She calmly watched their approach, as if she had expected them. When they reached her throne, the Dumonts bowed low and the other two followed their example.

Reginald Dumont called out:

"All hail Queen Seraphina of the Castle in the Sky!"

The young Queen rose from her seat, and Fritz had the thought suddenly that she was the physical embodiment of all the austere beauty of the buildings around them; she was the cold architecture personified.

"Rise, Reginald Dumont, and tell me why you come so late to your appointed place," said Queen Seraphina in a voice like sharp steel.

"Your Majesty, humbly I beg your pardon!" said Reginald, rising as commanded and immediately falling to his knees again.

"It is not my fault! Only listen and you will know that my tardiness is but the sign of greater fortune. For you see, I bring good news to you, my Queen!"

"What news is this?" said Queen Seraphina, taking her seat again and smoothing her dress uninterestedly, "I see that you bring your slobbering sycophant of a sister with you. Then, you have freed her sorry carcass from that prison, have you?"

"My Queen," began Bijou, but the dark-haired maiden cut her off with a cruel word.

"Silence! I spoke not to you, but to your brother. You weakling, keep your mouth shut. You, Reginald, answer me. What news will excuse your lateness?"

At these words, Reginald grabbed Fritz by the shoulder and hoisted him to his feet in front of the Queen. He pushed forward Florian the fox likewise. Then, he said:

"These are the two who will end the evil of civil war in the Lands Beyond the Moon."

Fritz held the gaze of Queen Seraphina as she peered deep into his eyes. She seemed to look through them, as if she searched his very mind. She smiled gently at the boy, and he felt strangely safe in her presence. The irritation she had shown toward the Dumonts was nowhere to be found in the smile that she offered him. To Florian as well, she turned a tender gaze.

When the Queen finally spoke to them, her voice sounded as awestruck and mesmerized as they felt.

"You…you come from beyond the Mountains of the Moon, from beyond the Milky Way…from Earth, don't you?"

"Yes," said Fritz and quickly added, "Your Majesty."

"Many long years I looked forward to your coming," said Queen Seraphina, "It is through you that Peace will be restored to the Vale and to all these lands. You must help me end this civil war between Whitlee and Goldburg, and bring Order to *my* realm."

Fritz looked at Florian, who nodded as if to say, "Go on, tell her."

The boy said:

"Your Majesty, we have come so far because we were told that we must help with tribulations here and drive evil from the Lands Beyond the Moon. I think this is exactly what she meant."

"She?" said Queen Seraphina, her eyebrows narrowing suddenly, "Who is she? Who told you this?"

"Hanna the shepherdess," said Fritz.

"Oh, Hanna!" said the Queen, her smile as wide as it could be now. She leaned back comfortably in her throne and said with a voice of contentment, "I am so glad you have met dear, sweet Hanna. She has not led you wrong. And of the things she spoke, I know much and will guide you from here. She was right when she said that you would drive evil from these lands."

"But how?" said Fritz, feeling so very small again, "How can Florian and I do this?"

"Why, you must kill the Fairy-Witch beyond the Ditch of Wyrms."

Chapter 19

"Kill her?" said Fritz and trembled suddenly with fright. This was a task for a brave warrior, not for a runaway boy. He did not want to face some horrible witch with power beyond imagining.

"Yes, kill her," spoke the Queen, "She is the cause of discord in these Lands Beyond the Moon. Her terrible strength helps those Whitlee fools and prolongs this awful war."

"But I do not want to kill anyone," said Fritz, "I did not come here seeking war."

"Yet you found war nonetheless," said Queen Seraphina, "You must kill her. It is the only way. Or else the men of the Vale will continue dying, year after year, in futile battles that accomplish nothing."

"But *how*?" said Florian suddenly, "How can we two do this thing, when all the power and might of your realm has not succeeded in it?"

As if in answer to the fox, Fritz remembered the words of that lovely golden-haired maiden, and he repeated them aloud now, "The smallest will be made great…"

Queen Seraphina's eyes grew wide at these words, and she leaned forward eagerly, clutching the arms of the throne, and said:

"Lo, a Mystery! As you have heard it spoken, so shall it be. Only look at me, my young travelers, if you doubt the words. I am small, meek in stature. Yet I rule from this mighty fortress. At my word, I give life and Death. At my word, I can make the mountains tremble, and the forests fall, and the clouds part. I am the woman Mystery, the smallest made great."

As she spoke, the Queen's voice rose in volume until the great hall echoed with her cries of power. Fritz and Florian wondered at the strength contained within this petite maiden, and her proclamations filled them with keen dread, not the holy fear as one feels in the presence of a righteous being, but the dire dread of something evil.

Fritz shivered. He did not know what to say and felt anxious in the presence of Queen Seraphina. He looked to Florian, who always seemed to stay calm in such a situation. The dread passed quickly from his foxy face and was replaced by a look of curiosity.

"Why haven't you defeated the Fairy-Witch yourself?" he asked, "Are you not a powerful sorceress?"

A quick whimper sounded from where the Dumont siblings knelt, as if they were frightened of the answer. Yet Queen Seraphina looked kindly at the fox, gave him a pat on the head, and said:

"A fair question, foxling. My magic is indeed great. I could bury the city of Whitlee beneath rubble if I wished…if not for the Fairy-Witch's defense of that place. And I could tear her apart with a word, except she has an even stronger shield against me, stronger than any black sorcery ever devised."

"What is that?" said Fritz.

"She is my sister."

Fritz took a step back in disbelief. He put his hand out to steady himself and found Florian's furry back.

"Your sister?"

"Yes, and no curse can kill a family member, no matter how much we wish the thing," continued Queen Seraphina, "She is covered by Sororal Protection, and no words of my magic can ever break through that. So it has ever been since the first killing was committed. If I wanted to kill her, I would have to do it by hand, by the sword, with brute force, as the first brother-murder was done. Yet my sister is filled with a Power greater than any magic. If it came to a physical fight, I am afraid that I could never win."

"But you expect us to defeat her by the sword?" said Florian.

"Yes, I do, fair fox," said the Queen, "You and the boy carry the power of Destiny with you. Your coming is as the thunder before the clouds break. This Earth child seeks the uttermost horizon, and he will find it beyond the Ditch of Wyrms."

Fritz felt his heart beat against his chest like a desperate prisoner banging at the walls of a cell. Fighting the Fairy-Witch was terrifying enough, but now this ditch sounded like certain death. Fritz knew what a wyrm was, and he had no wish to meet one.

"The Ditch of Wyrms is just a name, isn't it?"

"Oh, no, boy," said Queen Seraphina and waved away the thought with her delicate hand.

"It is a very real den of dragons in the mountains Westernmost. It is our one protection against the Fairy-Witch's invasion into the Vale. Her castle is on the other side of the ditch, and she will not cross over for the three dragons that live there. If the Fairy-Witch ever tries to come out of the West, the wyrms lie in wait for to devour her. You and the fox must sneak through that place, or failing that, you must defeat the three wyrms there named Groll, Zadza, and that most ancient one, Pycha."

Fritz felt like his small body would be crushed under the immense weight of such responsibility.

In all the longing of his heart, he had never expected to face such a task. He put his hand on the small dagger at his belt and shook his head.

"I am no warrior. I have no weapons, but this small knife. I am not ready to face three wyrms, much less the Fairy-Witch herself."

"Oh, but you are ready, boy," said the Queen. She raised her arms and clapped her elegant hands together in summons. "Or almost ready."

Immediately, a tall, stately man stepped into the hall. Engraved steel armor covered his body, and neat chainmail extended up his neck, but his handsome face was exposed. At his waist, he wore a sinister longsword, likewise engraved with fine carvings. He was clearly a man of some importance, perhaps a general of the armies of the Castle in the Sky. He was a young man, but apparently much experienced. Though handsome, his face bore scars that began just inside his right eye and cut across his nose at angles to the left side of his lip. This man-of-war knelt beside the Queen's throne with his hand placed over his heart.

"Your Worship," he said in a low voice.

"Lord Otto, take these two," said Queen Seraphina, motioning to Fritz and Florian, "And outfit them with arms. Give them weapons able to kill my sister and the deadly wyrms. They are come at last, the Peacemakers."

"As your Father said," spoke Lord Otto, but the Queen gave him a sharp look.

"Speak not of Him, as I have commanded. You try my patience, lord."

"Only out of love for Your Worship," said Otto.

"Bold talk, lord," said Queen Seraphina with narrow eyes, "And it is only out of my love for you that I spare your life for such impertinence. Say no more. Do as I bid. The Peacemakers need weapons."

Fritz listened to this exchange between the Queen and Lord Otto with much interest, but he did not understand what lay behind it. It struck the young boy as odd that so pretty a maiden as Seraphina could threaten execution for simply speaking as the lord had, and for speaking of her own father. Perhaps it was not odd at all, however; perhaps that was just how all queens were.

Certainly with a civil war raging Queen Seraphina had much to worry about, and maybe this was what made her so short with her subjects. Fritz hoped that he could help the cool, beautiful maiden, and bring Peace as she claimed. He caught Florian's eye, and read in the fox's expression that he, too, would embark on the dangerous task. He would not leave the boy's side. He would stay with him to whatever end.

"Now, go, you two," said the Queen. She paused and cast her eyes upon the groveling form of Reginald Dumont. A slight smirk spread over her pale lips as she said:

"And you, Dumont, you silver-tongued suck-up. So helpful were you in bringing them here, you will continue to accompany them on their quest."

"M-my Queen, m-maybe I should—"

"I have spoken."

"Yes, Your Majesty," said Reginald, and his voice sounded much smaller than usual.

Lord Otto motioned to a door on the north side of the hall, and Reginald walked that way followed by Fritz and Florian. Behind them, Bijou Dumont still knelt in front of the throne. As the group exited the throne room, they heard Queen Seraphina say:

"You foul, loathsome little creature. How could you get caught? You disgus—"

Then, the door slammed shut behind them, and they heard no more of the Queen's steely voice.

They passed through a short hallway into a long room, like a kitchen or servant's area where many lowly people, peasant and servants dressed in plain clothing, cowered away in the shadows of the room at the sight of Lord Otto. These servants bowed their heads as they went about their tasks, not daring to catch the eye of their superiors. Among their numbers were many folk who looked as if they were foreigners to the Castle in the Sky. There were creatures that Fritz

223

had only heard of in tales: satyrs and dwarfs and fauns and dryads and even a lonely-looking giant sitting in a corner milling corn with a giant stone mallet.

But most interesting of all was the flash of bright orange fur that caught Florian's eye, the full tail of a vixen that flicked and wagged in the gloom. She sat just behind a table, her face downcast as she went about her work, saying nothing and seeming to not even notice that anyone had entered the room. Florian smiled, for here was a beautiful vixen of the Lands Beyond the Moon, his heart's wish, and Fritz could tell that his friend wanted to leap at the sight. Though beautiful, there was deep sadness in her eyes, and as their group passed through the room, Fritz and Florian could both see that she wore a heavy iron chain around her back legs.

They said nothing to each other, but there passed a whole conversation of mutual understanding in their look. They continued to follow Lord Otto as he led them through a twisting maze of hallways to some deep inner armory.

When they came to the solid oak door, Fritz realized that the owl was still nowhere to be seen. In fact, he had not been in the throne room at all now that the boy thought of it.

He whispered to the fox so that no one else could hear, "Where is Hobs?"

But Florian only shrugged and said, "He flew away in the courtyard. I'm sure he will turn up somewhere."

Fritz thought it very strange for Hobs to go away before meeting the Queen of the Castle in the Sky, but then again he was an owl and owls know many things that young boys do not. He must have had a good reason for going off.

The door of the armory opened and Fritz's eyes were met with such an array of weapons as he had never seen in his life. Every kind of killing instrument you could ever imagine was contained in this room. Lord Otto told them to choose whatever they wished.

Fritz browsed through many menacing pole-arms, but all of them were made for grown men and far too unwieldy for him. A solid mace or bludgeon seemed a good fit for bashing at a dragon, but Fritz worried that it would not have a long enough reach. He would be roasted long before he could get close enough. Finally, after trying out many weapons, the boy settled on a razor-sharp, double-edged sword that he found light enough to swing with force, and yet sturdy enough to deal terrible damage.

Fritz also took a small steel helmet that fit snugly on his head, and a small shirt of mail that had been made for a boy just his size. He also helped Florian (who needed no weapon but his foxy teeth) put on some chainmail. The mail was a bit large; it had been made to protect a small pony. It looked a bit ridiculous on the fox.

"We will mend it to fit you," said Lord Otto, "I will have the smiths fashion a small champron for your head, fox, just as a war horse would have."

Florian thanked the man, while Reginald puttered around the room, dissatisfied.

"I do not wish for a weapon," said the small gentleman as he picked absent-mindedly at a bowstring, "I have no desire to strike a killing blow. Only let me speak with the Queen again. I am sure I would be better suited here. I can do much for the war effort that I cannot do if I go west."

"Stop talking, Dumont," said Lord Otto, "Just take a weapon."

Reginald mumbled to himself and kicked at the floor, but in the end, he selected a bevy of sinister-looking throwing knives. These knifes he wore strapped inside of his green vest.

The travelers thus outfitted, Lord Otto led them back into the hallways and said as they walked:

"You leave on the morrow. Now, Dumont, be gone to your room and rest up."

Reginald took his leave, still grumbling like a scolded child who had been told to go to his room with no dinner. To Fritz and Florian, the lord had a gentler voice as he said:

"You two will sleep in the loftiest tower. Come."

The spiraling stair that led to the room at the peak of the tower seemed to go on forever. Fritz wondered how many hundreds of feet he walked into the air. He had never been so high in all his life. Through arrowslits in the tower, he could see out over the whole of the gorgeous courtyards of the Castle in the Sky and over the walls to the sprawling city.

Finally, they reached the room at the top, and Lord Otto left them alone to settle down for the night. Fritz could not help but notice that he locked the door behind him as he left. The boy turned to the fox and said, "I am glad you're here, Florian, or I would be very frightened."

"I am frightened anyway," said Florian with a smile despite his words.

Fritz dropped his knapsack on the floor and breathed a tired sigh. He had carried that knapsack for many miles and still it contained all he had taken from his parent's cottage so long ago.

The fox walked to the window and added, "I wonder where Hobs has gone. He has been away for a long time."

As if in response to his question, the owl fluttered wildly in through the open window. He landed precariously on the chandelier hanging in the center of the round room, making it swing back and forth erratically.

From his perch, Hobs said, "*Hoo, hoo*, hallo, you two! How was the Queen then?"

Fritz raised his arm, and the owl leapt from the chandelier and alighted on it. The boy and the fox quickly explained all that had gone on and what they now faced.

"Dragons, eh?" said the owl, scratching his cheek with a talon as if considering a proposal, "I have heard of the Ditch of Wyrms only in vague tales, though I have never known anyone to see it and live."

"Then, you will not go with us?" said Fritz gloomily.

"*Ooo*, of course I will!" said Hobs with a sudden click of his beak.

"Where were you earlier?" said Florian.

"Exploring the castle. And I tell you, I found something disturbing, indeed."

"What is it?" asked the boy.

The owl shook his feathers and shivered all over as he remembered the thing. He looked suspiciously around the room and said:

"They have a withered old man in the dungeon here. An awful sight, and I do wish I had never seen him in such a condition. There was something great and dreadful in his ancient eyes. He must be quite hated to deserve the prison he was in."

"Well, why should that mean anything?" said Florian, "Many castles have prisoners in their

228

dungeons. Why should the Castle in the Sky be any different?"

"I do not know," said Hobs, shivering again, "But I do know that I would not like to get on the Queen's bad side."

Chapter 20

Fritz's dreams that night swam in the light of the pale moon, and everywhere he turned he saw the lonely figure of a suffering prisoner, an old man who had no name, or many names, and none that the boy knew. He wished that he could call out to the old man, who seemed to shine with a Light of his own, or free him from his bonds, but when the boy tried to take a step in the old man's direction, he found that he, too, was bound.

The bonds were tight, and Fritz had no power to even begin to loosen them. And the more he struggled to reach the man, the more the gap between them lengthened. An outer darkness was swallowing Fritz, as he was pulled away from the man of Light, and the boy began to despair that Death had come for him.

But the old man of Light did not struggle, or resist his bonds, but seemed to allow his own sufferings to continue unabated, and though blood began to run down his face as if his very brow had been pierced, still he did not turn away from the anguish of the sufferings. Almost as one glad did he accept them, as they grew more heart-troubling, until the very last forsaken moment, when he cried out, and there came a thundering sound as of rock cracking and of a veil rending, and the old man's face was upturned like a diver who, having descending into the darkest depths, now ascends to burst through the surface of the waters.

And suddenly there was a brilliant flash, and a trumpet shout, and Fritz bolted awake.

He lay in the room of the tower, breathing heavily, and much of the dream was quickly forgotten. The only thing that lingered was that strange feeling of helplessness, a feeling like bile at the back of your throat right before you are sick. It was a feeling that Fritz never wanted to experience again.

The boy shook the cold sleep from his body as he hopped out of bed. Florian lifted his head from beneath the blankets and they draped around his foxy head like an old woman's headscarf. High on the chandelier, Hobs snored with light *hoo, hoos*.

Fritz heard the lock turning in the door, and in stepped Lord Otto dressed in the flowing robes of a courtier, looking much more genteel than he had in his war armor yesterday. The scar on his nose still gave him a rugged appearance, despite the finery he wore.

Lord Otto carried the armor that the smiths had made for Florian and said, "As promised, fox."

He strode in and helped Florian dress in the chainmail. The lord fastened the champron to Florian's head, and the fox suddenly looked like a fierce warrior.

"You leave soon," said Lord Otto, "Dumont is already waiting on you. Get dressed, young one."

Fritz did as he was told, strapping the sword to his belt along with Father's dagger, and pushing the helm down on his head. Lord Otto turned and went down the stairs again, clearly expecting them to follow. He did not seem to have noticed Hobs, who now sat wide-eyed and awake on the chandelier.

"*Gohoo*, going already, are we?"

Fritz smiled and nodded, and the owl took his place on the boy's shoulder as they all followed Lord Otto out of the room.

Reginald Dumont sat outside on a half-wall of stone, morosely smoking his pipe. He looked rather glum and sleepy-eyed, as if he had been up most of the night. Imagine a schoolboy who has not studied for an exam and is suddenly awakened to be carted off to school, and then you have a fairly good picture of Reginald at that moment.

When they were all assembled, Lord Otto addressed them and said, "Leave through the west gate, and good luck to you. Succeed in ridding the Lands Beyond the Moon of the Fairy-Witch, and you will be lavishly rewarded. Fail and you will meet Death sooner than you wish."

Fritz did not find this a very comforting send-off, but Lord Otto had nothing else to say and turned to leave. As he did, the lord caught sight of the owl perched on Fritz's shoulder and took a quick double-look. His eyes lingered on Hobs for a second, and then with a scowl, he disappeared back into the Castle in the Sky.

"Nothing else to do but get this over with," said Reginald and took one last long puff of his pipe.

"Come, come, my good fellows," he added, and little clouds of smoke popped out of his mouth with each word.

So they all followed the small gentleman out of the western gate. The path ran as straight as an arrow shot to the edge of the floating sky-island, and there it ended suddenly. Fritz peered over the edge but only saw the feathery tops of clouds gliding beneath them.

"How will we get down?" said the boy, leaning far out over the edge.

"A good question that!" said Reginald, tugging at his coat and straightening his clothes as if primping to meet someone special. "I...um, well, there is only one way."

"And that is?" said Florian, also looking out at the wide emptiness below.

"Well, listen here," said Reginald, growing more nervous by the second. He coughed and rubbed the back of his neck, "As I say there is only one way. And seeing as how this whole enterprise depends on blind Faith, I do not think it should be surprising that it should begin like this. Why, my boys, don't you see?"

"A leap of Faith," said Fritz in sudden realization.

"Right you are, my boy," said Reginald, now clearly frightened, sweat running down his brow and his cheeks flushing red.

Florian laughed, nudged Fritz and said, "Well, what are we waiting for?"

And just like that, the fox leapt over the edge and disappeared into the clouds. Fritz laughed at the steadfast Faith of his companion. Then, he turned to the frightened figure of Reginald and shook his head. There was no way that the small gentleman was going to leap.

So Fritz pushed him.

The man plummeted over the edge with a startled cry and like a rock, plunged into the sea of clouds.

"Good one," said Hobs with a chuckle. Then, he dived through the sky and was gone.

Last of all, Fritz jumped over the edge and felt the world disappear beneath him as he fell through the cloudbank. He felt that sudden rush in his stomach that you know all too well if you have ever leapt from a very high place. For long seconds, he fell toward the land below, but felt no fear.

Just as the boy was about to smash into the ground, he felt as if all the weight went out of his body and he fluttered down on his feet as light as a falling leaf. With his feet firmly on the ground, he returned at once to normal.

"Ha ha!" he laughed aloud, "What a leap!"

The others had landed in the same way, and the little group found themselves high in the foothills of the Westernmost, the soaring mountain range that Fritz had seen earlier. The air had turned cold, and Fritz was glad for the wolf's skin coat that he still wore. It kept him warm despite the chill metal of his chainmail.

The young boy shouldered his trusty knapsack and led the way into the mountains. He knew what terror awaited him in this range, but that ditch was not yet entirely real to him. Still less real were the wyrms themselves, or worse yet the Fairy-Witch.

As they walked, Fritz suddenly heard on the wind those womanly whispers, just as he had heard so long ago in the Mountains of the Moon. He caught Florian's eye and knew that the fox recognized them as well. Although the boy knew he should be frightened, especially if they were the voices of fairies who bore allegiance to the Fairy-Witch, Fritz instead took great comfort in the strange chorus. The voices were still as unintelligible as they had ever been, but whatever they were, they did not seem malevolent or evil.

"Well, that's annoying," said Reginald, looking around them for the source of the noise. "I do wish they would say some intelligent, or else shut up."

"I wish the same sometimes," said Hobs, narrowing his eyes at the small gentleman.

But Fritz said nothing, only let the voices wash over him like a cool mountain rain as he walked. The feminine voices did not last long, their melody melting away into the whistles of the wind through the craggy rocks. The Westernmost made the Mountains of the Moon seem like anthills in comparison. The group marched and marched and never did the peaks seem to get any closer; still the summits were lost in the clouds, and the road endless.

"I wonder how far to the Ditch of Wyrms," said Florian.

"Not far enough," said Reginald, meekly. He seemed to know these parts well.

In fact, the small gentleman had been born in these very mountains, and as the group came around a curve of the road, he pointed far in the distance to the south. He traced a jagged line along mountainsides until he found a certain shoulder, and there was a note of sadness in his voice as he said:

"Over there is my ancestral home. I was born in the old Manor Dumont. But it has been long years since I or Bijou have been back."

Fritz strained to see, and he could just make out the shape of a mountainside estate, its stone walls catching the light of the sun as they seemed to spring organically from the rock around them. It looked a dreary and foreboding place to grow up, and it seemed little wonder to the boy that that house had produced the two rather unpleasant Dumont siblings.

"Does your family still live there?" said Fritz as they walked on.

Reginald was reluctant to answer for a few seconds, and then he said:

"No. It does not belong to our family anymore. Queen Seraphina seized it, and it serves now as a forward outpost to guard her northern borders."

"She took your house?" said Florian.

"My father was a most disagreeable fellow," said Reginald, still appearing quite uncomfortable with this conversation, "He...well, he supported the Fairy-Witch. In the end, Queen Seraphina had him...that is, he is not there anymore. And the Queen rightfully took the manor for her own use, as is her royal privilege."

"*Ooh*, oh, dear," said Hobs quietly.

For a long while after that, no one in the group spoke.

Past that cliff-side outpost, there came upon Fritz the realization that he was marching off to war. Of course, he had known this, but now he became acutely aware of the helmet pressing upon his brow, and the weight of the sword at his hip, and what exactly that weapon could mean in the days to come. He would live or die, and the difference between the two might be as thin as a hair split upon the sword's razor edge. Other creatures' and men's lives would likewise be decided.

As many boys do, Fritz has once harbored thoughts of heady glory to be won on the fields of battle. Yet he had seen exactly what such "glory" looked like on that meadow just outside of Whitlee; it looked suspiciously like indifferent bloodshed and uncaring death. How the soldiers had lain, slain and forgotten, no marker for their demise, no songs to their name, not even mourners who knew them. That is the end of battle, and once a man has tasted it, how hesitant he is to lift another spoonful to his lips.

And yet, that had been a pointless battle, a battle to prolong a meaningless war, seeking no end but itself; how could it not result in pointless death?

Here, in facing the wyrms and the Fairy-Witch herself, here was a chance to score a true victory, to face consequential war and to triumph over it. Never has there been anything as tempting, never a fragrance more enticing, than that of glorious victory just within reach.

It was with thoughts like this that Fritz led his fellow travelers high into the Westernmost. Deep within the mountains they pressed, where the shadows grew long though the sun was still up. The peaks swallowed the travelers up as if they were no more than the small snowflakes that fluttered down amongst them. Soon the tiny flakes built up into a true layer snow that swished and swirled, blown by the wind to collect in drifts on the sides of the path.

The travelers had been walking under the shade of tall pine trees that covered the lower mountains. Yet now, walled in on both sides by cliffs, the trees turned black and became twisted, charred trunks blasted by some unknown flames. These trunks seemed to stand as threatening markers, like signposts that pointed:

"This way to dragonfire. This way to the Ditch of Wyrms. This way to Death."

Fritz and the others passed beneath these burnt trees with growing unease. To either side of the road, the rock had been flashed into the glossy smoothness of obsidian and made the place look like the aftermath of a volcanic eruption. A sulfuric stench hung over the devastation, that rotten egg of brimstone.

"I say, I have n-never been this far into the W-Westernmost," said Reginald, "I f-fear we are perilously close to those infernal beasts."

He looked over his shoulder back to the safer East, but Florian nudged him forward. Fritz squinted to see into the distance ahead, but could make out nothing but the drifting smoke of smoldering embers.

"I think Reginald is right," said the boy, "We are close. The wyrms may come upon us at any moment. We must stay as quiet as possible now."

"Sound advice," said Hobs and fell silent.

The group stole cautiously through the blasted heath, watching every crag in the mountainside for hints of movement. But none appeared. This place lay heavy with the silence of fear.

At the far end of the flat space, the path ran up a sharp incline through a narrow opening in the rock and disappeared into the gathering darkness. The sun had fallen away ahead of them, taking the last comforting rays with it. Already the moon peeked through the sky, very small and far, far away.

Up the rise, the path appeared as if chewed by massive teeth and spit out into bits and pieces of scattered and jumbled boulders. The travelers picked and climbed their way over this disordered landscape. At the top of a particularly menacing stone, all misshapen with serrated and jagged edges, the group stopped and stood in hushed horror.

Below them lay the Ditch of Wyrms.

Chapter 21

A wide pit awaited them.

Like welcoming torches set on either side of an open gate, two blue flames of burning sulfur flickered to the right and left of them. Down into the ditch ran the road, and beyond these shining beacons, the place became an uneven basin of jutting rock and twisted tree trunks. The ditch yawned like the open mouth of some hideous rock-beast, an animal frozen in time with gaping maw, ready to devour any who dared enter.

Yet oddly there were many signs of life even in this foul place. Where the blasted heath earlier had been all burned and destroyed, this basin showed living evergreens, and flowering plants, and even a few carpeted patches of thick grass. And in the middle of it all twisted a river that watered the basin before flowing away behind them, east out of the Westernmost.

At the very far end, almost out of sight in the distance, this river entered the Ditch of Wyrms in a thundering waterfall that tumbled down from the great heights of the cliffs there. The sheer cliff face rose hundreds of feet into the air, and Fritz strained to see its top, wondering how they would ever climb it.

There would be time to consider the formidable cliffs later, however, because just now three deadly beasts lurked unseen somewhere. The wyrms must be dealt with before anything else. Fritz desperately hoped that he would just be able to sneak past the horrible dragons. Yet his little hand clutched the weapon at his waist, ready to draw the sword if necessary.

"Let's leave the road," whispered Florian, casting his foxy eyes around warily, "Perhaps we could pass safely by following the river to the falls."

"I-I say, fellows, what about splitting up?" stammered Reginald, "W-we don't want to be caught all at once."

Hobs nipped lightly at the small gentleman's ear and said, "*Doo, hoo*…do be quiet."

"No, I do not think splitting up is a good idea," whispered Fritz and crouched down to kneel in the road. He had spied a bit of movement far away in the murky north of the ditch. "They'd only kill us separately."

His eyes were still fixed on that place where he thought he'd seen movement, and now he was sure of it. A long, slithering black mass shimmered like metal as it descended from the heights and flowed over the rough rock like coursing mercury.

"I see one," said the boy breathlessly. His blood went cold, but he managed to give the order, "Quick now, to the river."

At the young boy's word, the travelers left the road at once and picked their way over the prickly landscape. They dropped down into the more protected river valley. At the water's edge, they took shelter beneath an evergreen left untouched by dragonfire. All four huddled together and hoped that the slithering wyrm had not seen them.

Fritz did not know which of the three dragons he had seen, but he did not wish to find out its name. The ditch fell silent now except for the distant roar of the waterfall and the flowing sigh of the river. The four travelers had just begun to breathe easily when another noise rose over the pit.

Chkka, chkka, chkka, it came, a raspy rattling noise that bounced off the rock and echoed throughout the place. *Chkka, chkka, chkka*. Quicker and quicker went the rattling until the shaking noise turned almost into a steady hissing flow like *chkkachkchchshhhh, shhhh, shhhh*.

"W-where is that coming from?" said Reginald, covering his ears and cowering in fear.

It was unlucky that the small gentleman covered his ears as he said this, because he spoke much louder than he should have at such a

245

moment. Almost as soon as he had spoken, the rattling stopped at once. The ensuing silence darkened the hearts of the four travelers for the knowledge that it brought.

The wyrm had heard.

"It came from over here," said a voice like a snake that had just learned to speak. The first word had a heavy *ish* sound, and the rest were spoken with odd pronunciations, so that the sentence came out more like this:

"Ish cahm frum ove hier."

And the strange voice punctuated its sentence with a quick *chka*.

The voice came from above them as they huddled in the hollow created by the river. The four of them squeezed back into the shade of the evergreen and crouched as low as they could.

"Do not answer back," whispered Fritz, as he clutched his knapsack tightly with one hand and drew his sword with the other.

Reginald had been struck dumb by fear, and so this command was unnecessary; the shivering little man could not have answered back even if he wanted to. Florian the fox sniffed at the air and whispered:

"It is in the middle of the road."

"You can hide by the river as long as you want. I will be waiting here," said the unseen wyrm as if in reply, that strange accent pricking like an arrowhead into the hearts of the travelers.

"When you are ready, I will kill you."

At this chilling pronouncement, Fritz exhaled. The dragon knew where they were; there was no sense in cowering nervously now. The idea that they could sneak through without a fight was gone. If there was any last lingering hope for sneaking, it disappeared completely when the voice of another wyrm hissed out:

"*Sss*-save *sss*-some *sss*-seared *sss*-slivers of flesh for me."

This second voice fell away into a hissing laughter, an eerie sneering punctuated by more of those heavy "s" sounds. Two of the beasts were now aware of their presence. The third dreaded creature remained unaccounted for, and this was perhaps worse than knowing the first two were out there.

There was nowhere safe to hide in the ditch, and there was no sense in waiting by the river to be eaten. The young boy raised his sword and said:

"We will have to fight."

The others did not look at all like they liked the idea, but Florian bared his teeth, ready to follow his friend's orders whatever they may be.

"H-how d-do you expect…I say, how do you expect to defeat such beasts? They are immortal!" stammered the panicky Reginald.

"Immortal?" said Fritz.

"Deathless!"

"But how will we ever get past them?"

Hobs clicked his beak and said, "Not by force of arms alone, my boy."

Fritz nodded and said, "There must be a way. Perhaps something in here can help."

He took his knapsack and began to rummage through its paltry contents. There did not seem to be any answer inside, however, only the bits of food that had gone uneaten, and of course, the three frosted scones that Fritz had taken from home so very long ago and that single leaf from the Great Oak that he had caught in the wild wood. There was also the Flame of Truth, shimmering with ruby rays as it reflected the stinking sulfur fires around them.

Fritz held up a sugary scone and said, "You don't suppose it is just hungry, do you?"

Florian smiled sadly and said, "Hungry, yes. But hungry to devour us."

"Well, I will not go without a fight," said the boy, replacing the scone in bag. He clinched his jaw and readied himself.

"Perhaps you might use the food to distract it," said Hobs with a voice like an old sage, "After all, distraction is the better part of warfare."

"W-worth a try," said Dumont, still shaking with fear. Then he added morosely, "We are going to die anyway."

"Come on, then."

Fritz took a link of cold sausage from the knapsack, left over from their traveling food supplies, and with sword in hand, he made for the road. As the group emerged from the river valley, they got their first clear look at the wyrm.

Now there are some things that must be understood about these beasts.

Though the wyrms of the ditch are sometimes referred to as dragons, these beasts are really quite different from what are now commonly called dragons, and what we would recognize as dragons. For one thing, they have no legs at all, and so resemble giant serpents more than any other common animal we know. Yet to call them a serpent or a snake is to distort their nature as a whole, because they are not very snake-like actually, except for having a bit of the Devil in them, as of course all serpents have.

And while these wyrms slither as snakes do, their skin is not reptilian at all. Its scales are much more like a fish's, and there are, in fact, gills just behind the powerful jaw through which the thing draws its wheezing breath. The scales of the wyrm interlock so as to form a sort of plate armor that could protect against even a thundering blow from a lance head delivered at high speed by a charging knight on a raging destrier.

And though the wyrmish body is long and serpentine, yet their skulls are much more like an ancient dinosaur's skull, or rather more bird-like and pointed. Their mouth forms almost a kind of a sharp beak that looks like it could slice through bone as easily as through parchment.

The last notable feature is the pair of great bat's wings that just now on the wyrm were folded over its back as it waited in the road. These wings are deceptive, for when folded they look miniscule and desperately out of proportion to the rest of the long beast. Yet when these are extended, the wingspan created is so great and the force generated by their flapping so powerful that it can blow over whole buildings, brick and mortar being nothing to them. In this way, the sluggish-looking beast, though fat around the middle, can achieve swift flight, fast enough even to outpace a peregrine falcon in freefall.

Just now as the group of travelers emerged on the road, the wyrm that met them was the great Groll, and it slithered back and forth impatiently on the jagged road. The wyrm was a quicksilver creature, its blackish serpentine form moving over the rocks and shining like that liquid metal as it flowed over the uneven ground. Suddenly the wyrm rose like a swelling wave and gathered its coiled strength beneath it, and a bristling mass of sinister-looking spines lifted on its head, like those feathered combs that certain birds display when they are agitated. Then came the awful *chkka, chkka, chkka* noise again, and Groll whipped its rattle tail to the left and it popped audibly, like the snap of a whip.

The wyrm spoke again, "Your blood will flow upon the rocks."

Its fiendish eyes locked on the boy that trotted toward it, and Fritz somehow found the courage to move forward and to hold that terrible gaze. When he was some twenty yards from the beast, the boy stopped with Florian at his side, Hobs on his shoulder and the frightened, crouching cowardly figure of Dumont behind him. The boy raised his voice and said:

"Stand aside and let us pass, wyrm."

"Silence, fool!" roared the beast with a sudden rumbling blast like a warhorn.

"You address Groll, Scourge of the Westernmost! Cower and beg for your lives, mortal. Hell-fire upon those who defy me!"

To drive this point home, Groll suddenly expelled a horrifying stream of dragonfire, spewing like a fiery geyser straight into the sky. The wyrm glared in hatred as the flames lapped at the cold air above it and then extinguished themselves.

"Put away your sword, boy. No man can kill me. I am one of the Immortals. Earliest among all the created. Older than the Moon and Earth. As ancient as the morning stars themselves. Like comets and lightning was our birth, and like them our Fall. And we have no end but Fire."

Groll roared again, shaking the roots of the mountains, such unfathomable fury bellowed from deep within the wyrm; from its dead heart thundered a terrible anger.

Yet Fritz did not blanch in fear or turn aside from his quest, but rather stood in defiance of the roaring creature. The boy knew that this may very well be his end, and that he might never again see the familiar world, not the home in which he was born, or the wild wood of his childhood, or the fields he knew, or all the pleasant stillness of a long and settled life. But such was the desperate ache, the unyielding hunger of his boyish soul, that all this seemed a fair price to pay for its fulfillment.

So he would not turn back; he could not, though he faced such a beast.

When the dragon saw that the boy would not run or beg for his life, it gave another roar, louder than the first if that were possible, so loud that it caused rocks to tumble from the precipitous heights. Then it sent swift tongues of flames at the boy and his companions, but they managed to leap aside from the scorching stream.

"I will satisfy my hunger on your bones."

Thus spoke the beast.

At that moment, Fritz took a hunk of salt pork and flung it toward the wyrm. The boy hoped that if the creature fell to eating, they all might be able to run around it and flee through the ditch.

Yet the wyrm caught the pork as it was still in the air, roasted it with a snort of fire, and swallowed the charred meat whole in one gulp.

"Mere appetizers for me," said the dragon, "It is kind of you to give me this, but I will still eat you."

"Of course, you will, O Great Groll," said Hobs suddenly in his most respectful voice. Then, the owl whispered urgently in Fritz's ear, "Throw something else to it. Quickly, boy."

Fritz obeyed and hurled a large chunk of cheese at the wyrm.

"Please eat all that we have to give," continued the owl with an exaggerated show of respect for the beast. Hobs had obviously gotten some idea. As Fritz tossed another morsel to the wyrm, Hobs said:

"We hope you enjoy them, and we wish you to know that we feel honored to be the main course for so magnificent and glorious a creature as Groll of the Westernmost."

"I say, owl, are you quite mad?" said Reginald, his face white with terror.

"*Shhoo*, shh, man," said the owl over his shoulder. To the wyrm, he said, "I declare, O Groll, accept these last morsels as tokens of our esteem."

Then, Hobs leaned in close to Fritz's ear and said very quietly, "Now give it the frosted scones."

The boy held up the first of the three sugary scones, and looked at it regretfully, thinking of how much Love Mother had put into baking them, how long he had saved them and how good they would have tasted in all their crumbly sweetness. Then, he tossed the treat to the wyrm.

Groll consumed the sweet scone greedily without even tasting it, and as the wyrm did this, something happened to it. It began to writhe and squirm as if in severe pain, as a common worm will do when you try to put it on your fish hook.

"What have you given me?" screamed Groll, that hideous beast, as it began to shrivel up like a withering flower.

"Another," said Hobs.

Fritz threw another scone, and though the wyrm looked as if it wanted to avoid the morsel with all its strength, some gluttonous part of it could not help but eat the thing. And more pain racked its body as it did so, and the wyrm cried out:

"No more. No more! These reek of mother-love! They are tainted by it. They burn my innards. Stop it! No more!"

"One more," said the owl in his wisdom.

The boy tossed the last of the scones to the beast, which by this time had shrunk to the size of a small python and its bat wings had turned to something like wrinkled, wet parchment.

The wyrm seemed to have no choice but to eat the frosted scone. As soon as it did, it wriggled away from the road in considerable pain and lamenting for the loss of its greatness.

"Curse Love and all who have it."

For, you see, wyrms have no Love, and will never know what it is to Love truly, despite their long immortality. It is in this way that they have a little of the Devil in them, as mentioned earlier.

So Groll, Scourge of the Westernmost, vanished into the darkness, but there were still two more wyrms to face.

Chapter 22

The next wyrm, Zadza, awaited them down the road. This scarred and demented creature wanted to char and devour the travelers even more than the first beast had; its entire body seethed with a craving for flesh.

There were no more scones that could sate this wyrm.

The hissing beast skittered over the uneven ground toward them, moving like a millipede on a thousand tiny legs too small to be seen beneath its heaving mass. Where Groll had had a beak for a mouth, the new terror of Zadza had great fangs like the chelicerae of some awful spider, or the mandibles of an insect that creeps through the darkness of your dreams.

With every hiss of its breath came blasts of smoke and flame snorting from its nostrils. The dragon had spied Fritz first, for the prize of a child is supreme in the minds of such evil beings, and all else fades away when there is an opportunity to devour innocence. For this reason, the wyrm ignored Florian and Hobs, and most of all poor, cowardly Reginald Dumont, who was the furthest from innocence of the whole lot.

Zadza eyed Fritz alone.

The right eye of the wyrm worked fine, but the left eye socket of the beast was a twisted and gnarled chunk, like the smashed exoskeleton of a cockroach caught under the heel of a boot. The wyrm had suffered this injury sometime in the long, innumerable years of its life, and the various other scars and gashes in its sleek body told of countless other horrors it had encountered or caused during its time.

Watching the travelers approach with its one good eye bulging and bloodshot, Zadza licked its wretched lips.

"*Sss*-so *sss*-small and ea*sss*ily eaten," said the wyrm, clicking its sharp claws on the stone. It followed this awful noise with one worse, a sort of slimy laughter that hissed and steamed like a tea kettle left too long on the fire.

Fritz held his sword firmly, ready to fight the deadly wyrm with all the strength in his body, even though he knew deep down that it was futile to match strength against such a beast. Florian stood next to the boy, and every orange hair on the fox's body stood on end, as his growls rumbled with such wildness that Fritz could hardly believe such sounds came from his normally tame companion.

Poor Reginald Dumont, for his part, fell flat on his face in the middle of the road and lay prostrate as if groveling before the great beast, crying and shaking with the profound fear and debasement that only a coward can ever know.

"Oh please, oh please, oh…" was all the little man could say.

There is no use pleading for mercy from a wyrm, any more than there is pleading with the sun not to rise. Yet, it did not matter one way or the other what Dumont did, because Zadza's hatred was focused solely on the boy. The small gentleman, along with the fox and the owl, were utterly forgotten as the dragon's single eye fixated on the boy with a consuming hunger that bordered on insanity.

"You will not essscape," sneered the wyrm.

Still Fritz said nothing, but this was not out of fear. Fear was a foreign thing to such a boy in moments as these; he broke into a run toward the beast with silent determination. When he was a stone's throw from the wyrm, Hobs the owl said suddenly in Fritz's ear:

"Wait!"

Hobs repeated this and many other phrases meant to slow the boy down, for the owl had seen something which the boy had missed and which filled the owl with dread. When he saw that Fritz would not slow his pace but still barreled on, the owl leapt from the boy's shoulder, just as Zadza whipped its massive tail around like a scorpion and stung the boy straight in the gut.

For it was this that Hobs had been trying to warn of, this deadly weapon poised to strike.

Fritz cried out in pain, but he did not realize just then how grievously he had been injured or how dire his situation had suddenly become. When he looked down at his gut where the poison had entered, the wound appeared quite minor, especially considering the force with which it had been delivered. After stinging him so quickly, Zadza retreated up a boulder-strewn hillside, much like an insect skitters away when the torchlight reveals its position. Fritz fell to his knees, watched the beast move away, and pressed his little hand over the wound.

When he brought his hand up, there was no blood on the palm and he felt relieved for a few fleeting seconds. Perhaps the chainmail had turned aside the barb of the creature's sting, he thought. Perhaps he was not hurt after all. But when he raised the mail shirt, there was a black spot about the size of a coin, a hole in his belly, and around it like bolts of lightning shot jagged streaks of blackness as the corruption coursed through the boy's veins.

"Oh, dear," said the owl solemnly as he alighted on the boy's shoulder again, for in his wisdom, the bird knew how badly the boy had been hurt.

You see, the worst thing about such a sting was that it was not fatal. The boy did not know at that moment, but Zadza's venom would not kill him; even if he was never treated and did nothing to care for himself, he would go on living for just as long as he would have had he never been wounded at all.

The power of the poison was not in death, but in taking all the happiness out of life. It pollutes everything; it creeps into every part of the body and to every aspect of life until it has killed everything worth living for and yet left the body still persisting in its deadness. It would take the feeling from his skin, until all was numb. It would take the taste from his mouth, until sand and bitter heat were all he would know. It would take the laughter of his heart and turn it to insatiable hunger and self-loathing. It would spoil the longing of his soul into perversion.

And last of all, when it seemed there was nothing left to ruin, when it seemed all was lost, it would turn his own eyes into instruments of torture, for everywhere the boy looked he would see the reminders of his past life, and the relics of his ruined innocence, and the happiness and joy that could never again be his, and finally the interest would accumulate on his bankrupt soul until all hope of purity and holiness were lost in the long years of a half-life.

Yet as mentioned before, the boy did not know any of this.

And it was a very good thing that he did not. Hobs the owl knew, and only much, much later would he share it with the boy, who thanked the owl for not telling him at the time, for panic and fear would surely have defeated him.

So it was lucky then that Fritz only thought he had received a minor flesh wound from the wyrm. For he had the courage and strength to stand again and fight on. Had he known what he faced, he might have ended up a cowardly wreck like whimpering Reginald Dumont.

Hobs took to the sky again, as Fritz ran up the hillside mostly undaunted and aware now of the danger posed by dragon's deadly tail. When Zadza hissed and swung the tail around again, the boy was ready this time and ducked. The tail whistled past harmlessly. When he reached the beast, Fritz hacked at its body, but the sword, sharp though it was, did nothing against the wyrm.

Florian was at his side now and leapt on to the beast, his sharp teeth searching for an opening in Zadza's defenses. Yet though the fox bit and bit and tried to injure the wyrm, all his efforts did nothing. The dragon shook its massive body like an animal emerging from water, the exoskeleton clicked and rattled like plate armor from the shivering motion, and the fox flew into the air as an orange blur.

"Your friend*sss* cannot help you."

Fritz dodged another strike, and hacked again at the belly of the beast, hoping to catch it in a soft spot there. Yet the belly was as rigid and impenetrable as the creature's back, and the blade turned violently aside, giving Fritz such a rattling shock that his whole body vibrated from the collision, like a tuning fork.

The wyrm reared back, rising to a great height as it readied for the killing strike, and Fritz thought that he had been beaten. The boy was ready to drop the sword and accept his death, but just then, Hobs swooped past him and cried:

"The eye! The eye! Blind his right eye! Stab it! Pluck it out! Throw it away!"

Then, the owl caught the wind and swept upward on the wing and flew out of sight.

It was the only chance. As the great wyrm fell at him, Fritz took the Great Oak leaf from his knapsack and tossed the leaf into the air. By some Grace, it covered the beast's eye like a blindfold. For a moment, the wyrm could not see, and Fritz took his sword, aimed for the bulbous eye under the leaf and jabbed upward with all his strength. There was a horrific sound of popping like a ripe fruit smashed against stone, and then the scream of the dragon.

"*Sss*-sight, oh *sss*-sweet *sss*-sight!"

Zadza wriggled back and forth in that grotesque nervous motion that you will know if you have ever had to behead a snake. The head may be gone but the death throes persist. This wyrm was not dead, however, for you must remember, such beasts are deathless. Zadza seemed only to shrink in size, much like Groll had withered, and with uncontrollable spasmodic movements, Zadza rolled off the hilltop and disappeared amongst the scattered rocks.

Fritz had cast down the second wyrm, but the poison was still in his body.

The young boy slipped and slid back down the hillside to the road, and fell into a heaving heap, struggling to catch his breath as the black lightning in his belly spread its bolts deeper into his blood. The poison tickled — this is a strange word to use, yes, but there is not any other word that could come close to describing exactly what the boy was experiencing just then, so tickle will have to do — tickled as it flowed throughout his body.

Perhaps it is understandable in this way: have you ever had a bruise that you could not stop poking? It is not necessarily that you enjoyed the pain (or is it?) but for some reason you found yourself continually pressing your finger into the bruised spot, knowing full well that it would not help the healing process and knowing also that it was rather a silly thing to be doing, and yet...it was strangely enjoyable in its odd, stupid way. Perhaps this is how the pain in the boy was, and why he might have said that it tickled.

This is the worst thing about poisons and deadly sins—that we enjoy them.

When the boy finally managed to pull himself up, the others had crowded around him in sympathy and Florian nuzzled him gently with his kind nose. The fox was enough of a friend to know not to speak to Fritz, for there are moments when merely the presence of a friend is worth much more than words.

What could words do for the poison in his belly anyways? What words can staunch a wound?

As the group of travelers knelt in the middle of the road, the third wyrm came to them in silence. The last of the ancient beasts stole through the night and slipped effortlessly down from the high branch of a pine tree to land on the boy's shoulder.

The wyrm was called Pycha, and it was no bigger than a finger's length.

Chapter 23

Smooth and slick, easily missed and deadly in its seeming smallness, the wyrm Pycha wiggled dangerously close to Fritz's ear and began to whisper.

The words and the sayings that the beast whispered were of utter darkness and depravity, but they started so meekly that at first the boy did not even realize that he was hearing them. The sayings began gently, almost imperceptibly, and the words seemed to come from somewhere within Fritz's own mind, so that the boy believed at first that they were his very own thoughts.

The words went something like this:

"Lift your head up. The horizon is calling you."

You see, that is not something that would have been strange for Fritz to think on his own. This is why the boy did not realize what was happening at first.

The wyrm continued to whisper:

"Fear not. What is fear to one like you?"

"Lift your head, Fritz. You are Strength. Your body is a temple. And your mind is god."

"Have no fear. Look upon yourself. What do you see? Wonder and glory, everlasting and forever."

"Do not think lowly of yourself when you are so beautiful. You are the one. The best of all living. You are greater than the great I AM, for you are the great *I*. Why should you hang your head when you are Man, whose mind is god?

"Look upon yourself only. Who are the others? Who is anyone in the face of a god? There is no one above you, Fritz. All are nothing in the presence of you, you alone."

These were the things which the wyrm said, and they meant little to Fritz who had never spent much time thinking about the goodness of himself or comparing himself to others. The young boy had no reason to believe such lofty things about himself and did not at first accept them. Yet now that the wyrm had planted these seeds of thought in the boy's mind, the beast began to water them with proof.

"Remember your flight from the wolves. Remember how you swam the Milky Way. Only a god could cross the stars with such ease."

Do not wonder that the dragon could know these things about Fritz without being told them. Somehow our dragons, our devils, our tempters always know the most personal things about us;

sometimes they seem to know them better than we know them ourselves, and such was the case with the wyrm Pycha and the young boy. The dragon went on:

"Remember how you escaped the Shadows in the Mountains of the Moon."

Of course the wyrm left out the unflattering bit about disobeying the advice of the Watcher and conveniently forgot about how the strange stone had rescued them with the saving Grace of its blue rays.

"Remember how you got past the walls of Whitlee," said Pycha, forgetting about all the help Reginald Dumont had contributed in that endeavor.

"Remember how you freed the Dumont woman and escaped the prison," whispered the wyrm, leaving out the facts of the black magic that had saved them in that case, magic that thankfully had nothing to do with the young boy.

"Remember your feats in the gnome pits and your trickery with the Bog King," said the wyrm, ignoring how much had been done there by Florian the fox.

And on and on went the wyrm as it spoke tales of glory in the boy's ear and stoked his ego with the power of a blacksmith's bellows, whispers like blasts of air that fanned the flames of self-worth until they grew into the infernos of narcissism. There were other things too that the beast whispered, things so vile that they cannot be repeated here.

The point is when the boy raised himself up to stand straight, he felt quite confident. He had completely forgotten about the poison in his belly. How could he think of something bad within him when all his thoughts were bent to his own goodness? A man who thinks so highly of himself will hardly have time to dwell on his faults. Fritz thought he was perfectly fine, better than fine.

He was a god.

The wyrm had told him so.

"We must go on," he said to his fellow travelers.

The others marveled at the sudden change that had come over Fritz. The boy had gone from whimpering in the despair brought on by the venom to suddenly standing proud, ready to press on. None of them had noticed the wyrm Pycha yet, for it was no bigger than an earthworm, and it clung to the boy's ear, slick and gray and formless.

"Are you able to go on?" asked Florian tenderly.

"I am more than able," said Fritz, feeling the strange tickle of venom pumping through him, but ignoring it for the tickling in his ears.

"More than able," he repeated, "I am a god. I am Me."

"*Yoo-hoo*, you are you," said Hobs, slipping into the language of the owl as he did sometimes when he was thinking hard on something, "*Toohoo*, that is true. But what does that have to-*hoo* do-*hoo* with anything?"

"Do not question me, beast," said Fritz, raising a hand as if to strike the poor bird, "I am Man, and I am the great I."

"Man? I?" said Florian, not fully understanding, and hurt by the harsh words of his friend, even if they were not directed at him.

"I do not need you underlings," said the boy, "You only hold me back. I will press on and you may follow if you wish. I care not."

Fritz began walking into the West, leaving the other three standing open-mouthed in the middle of the road.

"I do not need friends…"

The look on the fox's face when the boy said this was the look of a heart breaking, and it is a look that you should hope you never have to see. He loved the boy, loved him with all the simplicity of a true friend, and this was the hardest of all sayings for such a friend to hear. Florian could do nothing but follow, as heavy teardrops formed in his trembling eyes.

Reginald Dumont went along with plodding footsteps, finding nothing especially odd about the boy's sudden change in behavior; Dumont had never thought much of other people anyway and so he was apt to agree with the boy's saying. Hobs followed as well, his wise owlish face scrunched in concentration as one trying to figure out a rather difficult riddle.

"What about the other wyrm?" said Dumont weakly and fearfully as they headed to the other side of the pit.

"I fear no others. What are others to Me?" said Fritz, never looking anywhere but forward, his back straight and his chin held high and his nose pointed to the sky.

Meanwhile Florian cried the silent tears of betrayal.

But Hobs hooted and hopped suddenly, because he had seen the root of this evil. The owl had noticed the slimy gleam of the little wyrm's skin where it perched beneath the boy's ear.

"The wyrm! The wyrm! Oh, my boy, it is on you!"

Florian's head jerked up, and the tears of his heartache dried at once and flamed into the fire of renewed friendship, for his best friend was in danger of death and that trumped all else.

"The wyrm Pycha!" cried the fox, "We must destroy it!"

"But it is so small," said Dumont, not as afraid as he had been of the other two dragons. There did not seem anything particularly dangerous about something so small, not compared with the two massive monsters they had already defeated.

Yet when Florian leapt to defend Fritz, the wyrm showed just how dangerous it could be, as it wiggled into the ear of the boy and disappeared inside his head. There would be no fighting it now, not by force anyway, not if they wanted to save Fritz's life.

Fritz did not react to the wyrm entering his ear, but continued to behave with the conceited superiority that he had assumed when the beast began whispering of his greatness. The pride in his head seemed only to make the poison from Zadza flow quicker through his veins. Yet the boy did not seem to feel pain or to fear death, even though death was quickly taking him from the inside out. All the color went out of his cheeks, and all the life seemed to drain from his body, but still he persisted in pride and arrogance.

"There is nothing to fear," he said to the others, ignoring their cries, "I am invincible. I alone will vanquish the Fairy-Witch. All others are nothing before Me."

But these were not the words of the boy. They were the words of the wyrm in his mind.

It is very likely that had Hobs the owl not worked quickly to intervene, the voice in the boy's head would have either driven him mad or else compelled him to do things that would have quickly brought about his own death. Overconfidence makes people do what they would normally call insane, and the wyrm had pushed Fritz to the heights of arrogant pride.

"Me, Me, Me," were the words in Fritz's mind, and soon these would have spread everywhere inside of him, to the depths of his heart and even to the bottom of his very soul.

It was good fortune then that Hobs had another of his splendid ideas.

"You must ignore it," said the owl in his wisdom, "You must not listen to the wyrm. Its words bring death. You must simply ignore what it says."

Fritz was walking to the edge of a precipice, below which was a hole full of jagged rocks. The boy walked as a dog led by a master, having no will of his own.

"Ignore the wyrm! You must not listen."

"Fritz, please!" cried out Florian, "Oh Fritz, my friend! Do not listen to the wyrm."

Fritz stopped at the cliff's edge. His death waited below, waited only for him to follow the last instructions of the wyrm:

"Leap. You are a god. You cannot be harmed. Leap and your mind will soar."

The boy did not leap, though, for a very simple reason. The reason was that he heard the voices of his friends, especially the kind, soft voice of Florian the fox, calling out to him.

You see, it is enticing to believe that you alone are wonderful, that you are an individual who needs no one else, that you are better than everyone else. But in the end, it is a very lonely — and a very *false* — belief, and it would be a very lonely and cheerless life even if it were true. Friends are the great cure for such an affliction, and friends were certainly the salvation in this instance.

For it was the voice of a friend that held him in place, as Fritz tried desperately to listen to the owl's advice and simply ignore the wyrm in his head. Still Pycha filled him with thoughts of his own superiority — an intoxicating drug and one hard to resist — but Fritz tried to block it out. It was difficult at first, and the more he tried, the fiercer the wyrm assaulted his senses.

This went on until Fritz slipped into a peaceful state of mind, content in the realization that he had friends who loved him and that he was no greater than they, and they no greater than he, and Love above all was the greatest. This was the first victory. The second victory was maintaining this mindset against renewed attacks by the wyrm, until at last, the dreaded creature inside the boy's head began to be defeated.

This defeat started with the wyrm falling out of his ear, apparently expelled by its failure to break the boy. Once outside the boy's body, the wyrm thrashed about as it weakened and weakened under Fritz's passive resistance and before the face of real friendship.

"You are a fool not to listen!" screamed the wyrm in terror and desperation.

But the opposite of this seemed to be true, because the more Fritz did not listen, the weaker the wyrm became. The creature flopped and squirmed around like an earthworm in the mud, but all its power over the boy was lost.

Soon the wyrm began to feed on its own words, swelling its own pride with false assurances and lies of superiority. As the wyrm swallowed more and more of its own lying words, it went mad. It swelled and swelled and swelled, like a balloon being overinflated by an overambitious child. Its smooth wormy skin stretched and stretched and stretched, and changed colors from deep gray to almost white, until at last when the stretching could not go on anymore, it popped!

A violent and thunderous explosion burst out, and the wyrm screamed out in pain as it was viciously thrown by the force of the explosion into the air and came down in a shattered heap in the ditch of rocks. Although it did not die, the wyrm named Pycha was vanquished and fled from the boy Fritz.

The Ditch of Wyrms had been conquered.

Chapter 24

The West beckoned them onward, and the end of their adventure drew near. The Fairy-Witch waited in her fortress.

Fritz insisted that the group walk to the western end of the ditch before he would allow himself a rest. The boy wanted to reach the waterfall as quickly as possible. When the travelers reached the misty falls, they found a small, but welcoming stretch of greensward that had escaped the ravages of dragonfire.

Here they rested. Fritz fell upon the ground and felt the spongy grass on his face and inhaled deeply the fresh soil scent. It was rather like collapsing into one's favorite chair at home at the end of a long day.

The boy and his companions stayed for a little while, none of them speaking and Dumont finding some time to have a nervous smoke of his pipe. The rushing plunge of the icy water, a continuous roaring rhythm, worked to soothe their tense bodies and comfort their minds that had been on edge since they entered the ditch. All of them were content in the present moment, except for Dumont who seemed increasingly anxious and ready to bolt as he puffed on his pipe and thought of the Fairy-Witch.

And though the boy sighed and enjoyed his rest for a moment or two, Fritz still had the poison of old Zadza coursing through his veins. The more rested he became, the more he began to turn his mind to the task that still faced them, and the more Fritz began to wonder how he could ever have the strength to battle the Fairy-Witch while the venom of that terrible wyrm filled his body.

He did not mention this to his companions, because he knew there was nothing that they could do for it. The boy saw no sense in worrying them. He would only have to redouble his own efforts, grit his teeth, and press on. His friends could not do this for him, so why even let them in on the struggle?

When the time came, Fritz looked through the fog to the top of the falls and said:

"We must go up."

Florian had been waiting for this command, and he pointed his snout to an outcropping of rock and said, "There seems to be a stair. A way up."

"I say, gents, do we have to?" said Reginald, stowing his pipe, "It strikes me now, well, that is…I should think that we might be able to just…go away. Let us go back and strike out for the Trackless Wood, and *hide*. Then we would not have to face the Fairy-Witch…or the wrath of Queen Seraphina when she finds out what we have done. That is to say, what we have *not* done…"

Hobs ruffled his feathers and shook his whole body as if these words made him physically uncomfortable, and Florian said:

"How can you say such things? Have you no courage? Are you just all words, and more words? Talk yourself to death if you like, but I will go on by Fritz's side. Unto whatever end."

Fritz pressed a hand over his wounded belly, smiled feebly at the fox, and whispered, "Thank you."

Then the boy headed for the natural rock stair that twisted up the cliff side and said over his shoulder to Reginald, "Come on, you. There is no going back."

So they went up and up and up, over the rough, uneven stone steps slick with the mists of the waterfall. Higher and higher into the peaks of the Westernmost their journey took them, until at last they reached to the top of the falls and emerged on a wide plateau.

Before them stretched a flat expanse of land, but it was not an empty or dead rock plateau as one might expect at this height. Rather it was a smooth stretch of lush garden brimming with abundant green life and flowering plants and watered all throughout by the mountain river.

And if you traced the line of this river farther to the West, you would end up at a water gate in the base of a mighty white citadel, the home of the dreaded Fairy-Witch. This gate was far off yet, across the fertile high plain, and it was closed and barricaded by a sturdy portcullis.

Behind the gate soared the heights of the fortress, like a three-tiered wedding cake, all white and pearly, and the tiers tapering toward the top to magnificent spires that looked so dainty and thin that they might have been made from sugar. The heights of the buildings were crowned with the spikes and spires and arches and flying buttresses of Gothic cathedrals. This gave it all over a spindly and sinister quality, as if its ramparts and roofs were all lined with lances and spears against any invaders who might be silly enough to try to lay siege.

As he stood staring across the rich plain at this dominating fortress, Fritz saw how impossible his task was. The Fairy-Witch of such a stronghold could not be assaulted by four of the finest soldiers in the universe, much less by a young boy, a fox, an owl, and a miserable coward.

Yet Fritz wanted to help Queen Seraphina to end the civil war. Was this not the prophecy made by the shepherdess Hanna that he and Florian were to bring an end to evil? Surely this

Fairy-Witch must be killed, and the seeming impossibility of that task only made it all the more necessary that it be done. Fritz marched forward. Courage and hope would have to see them through. There was no turning back.

A sign stood before them, and it read "The High Road." The travelers marched up this High Road directly toward the main gate of the Fairy-Witch's fortress. Narrower and narrower became the road, and arrow-straight was its perilous course, and not many could walk it. The whistling of song-birds played a marching melody, and it was strange to see such peace and life living in trees that grew in the Fairy-Witch's shadow. How was it that such a one had not destroyed such beauty? It did not make sense that an evil witch should rule over such a beautiful mountain sanctuary.

"This all must be a spell," said Fritz after some time, "All fake, all nothing. How else could a witch live in such a perfect garden?"

"The power of the Fairy-Witch is beyond comprehension," said Reginald, fearfully, "I have heard tales that she has knowledge that defies all understanding. And she guards her secrets like precious gemstones."

Fritz was reminded suddenly of the prized ruby that was hidden still in his knapsack, but said nothing. They drew close to the fortress of the enemy. The high curtain wall reared up in front of them like a towering wave of white water. The whole place was built of the purest white stone, or else all white-washed to seem pure.

"The Fairy-Witch," whispered Reginald, growing more frightened in the shadow of the wall, "She has a disgusting affinity for those rebels in Whitlee. See how her walls are white like theirs, or theirs like hers, I should say. It is her help that sustains their fighting, and it is for Love of her that the Whitlee scum endure."

"She must be an awful woman," said Fritz.

"She is no woman at all," said Dumont, "She is something grander and more terrible."

Now the very gates of the Fairy-Witch stood before them, and the time had come. The mighty gates were closed fast, and there was no sign of life on the high ramparts or in the turrets on the wall. The place was somehow dead and watchful at once, lifeless and yet Fritz could feel countless living eyes upon him.

It was an odd feeling to stand here at the end of all things, and to feel so small.

The gate was impenetrable, and they had no hope to storm the citadel with such a measly company. But Fritz knew at once what he must do. He knew it as if he had known it all along, as if he had been rushing toward it his whole life and now he was finally at the fated moment.

He alone must face the Fairy-Witch.

"This is why I came here," said the boy quietly to the fortress, and the other three stared at him in wonder, "To face her alone."

"An interesting idea," said Hobs.

"You are crazy, boy!" said Reginald.

"It is the only way," said Fritz. The decision had been made, and the others knew they could do nothing to sway the boy. His face told them all that he was ready to face whatever he must, to cast out evil from the Lands Beyond the Moon, to satisfy his aching soul.

Now Fritz raised his voice and cried out to the fortress:

"I have come for the Fairy-Witch! Let her come out and fight! Let justice be done for her evil!"

His voice sounded tiny before the mighty citadel, like a feather thrown against a mountainside. For long seconds the only answer was silence. The boy called out again:

"I seek the Fairy-Witch that I may cast her down! Come and face your end!"

Again there was no answer except for the heavy silence that filled the place in the absence of Fritz's voice. Then, without warning, came the reply.

A mighty trumpet blast shook the roots of the mountain, and shook the bodies of the companions to their very hearts, and shook the stars in the sky until they trembled in the blackness, and the clouds rolled away. The terrible note reverberated and hummed on the air, and made the night alive with tremulous fear at its awesome sound. When at last the note seemed to be dying away, there came another blast, louder and longer than the first, and Fritz had the distinct thought that the mountains would crumble if it went on one second more.

Then, just as suddenly, silence fell back upon them like a breaking wave.

And the gates of the fortress flew open.

The Fairy-Witch stood silhouetted in the white space, her form defined by a blinding brightness that flooded out behind her. She strode forward with soft, silent steps, her arms folded in front of her in flowing folds of white silk. She was clad in white from her delicate face to her graceful feet, and on her pale brow she wore a pearly diadem that shimmered with white light. All was purest white, except for the brilliant blast of color that sprung forth in wavy locks of reddish hair piled high on her head like a bubbling fountain of fire.

She was terrifying in her stark beauty, and if Fritz had not been so ready to fight her before the gates opened, he had the sudden feeling now that he might have fallen down and worshiped her. She was upon him already, and she seemed to know the boy's thoughts because she said in a voice like sharp diamond:

"Peace, be still. Do not worship *me*! I am but a servant. See how I stand in the Light. But I am not the Light."

Fritz and the others fell dumb at these words and at the voice of the one who spoke them, and if there had still been any notion of fighting left within them, they might have claimed that the words were a cunning trick or a deadly spell to make them unable to fight. Yet all thought of battle had fled at her appearance, and the others, like Fritz, stood in awed silence.

The woman in white spoke again, saying:

"Why come you here arrayed for war, and why call you out pronouncements of death and justice upon me? Whence came hatred between us, and why do you seek my downfall?"

Yet Fritz still could not speak, but rather fell to his knees at her pearly voice, ringing with the pure Light beyond and the note of the trumpet that still echoed in the boy's head. On his face was written holy fear, and his eyes were upturned to the Utter West, to the peaks at the End of Everything, and his heart's cup filled to overflowing with the Light.

The woman in white smiled down at the boy and said, "I have had word of you, child, you who comes from beyond the Mountains of the Moon, the wandering boy from Earth."

Here the magnificent being bowed her own head low in respect and said, "I am humbled and honored to meet you finally, boy, and I welcome you here with all kindness."

"But...but..." said Reginald Dumont, the first to find his voice, "But we are supposed to defeat her...she is evil...she is the Fairy-Witch—"

"Silence!" said the woman in a voice like thunder, but completely without cruelty or hostility. Reginald cowered and fell on his face.

Fritz pulled himself to his feet at last with a great effort and said, "We were told to kill you. That you were the evil that infected the Lands Beyond the Moon. But you...you are beautiful."

At these words there came a loud chorus of giggles from within the fortress and from the ramparts and battlements on high. The woman in white said nothing, but smiled humbly.

Fritz and his companions looked around in confusion for the source of the feminine laughter, but none could be seen.

The boy said with wonder:

"Who are you?"

This was met with yet more laughter, tinkling on the air like the ringing of many tiny bells. Louder and louder came the laughter in waves of merriment and joy. This went on until suddenly the gates flung open again and there sounded another mighty blast of the trumpet and the army of the fairies marched out in all its splendor and majesty. The dreadful hosts came forth.

In that same moment, the great ruby called the Flame of Truth began to burn brightly with the heat of a thousand suns and burst from the knapsack with a searing Light.

The red gemstone fell at the feet of the beautiful being.

The woman in white smiled broadly now, as she stooped to take up the ruby, and she said:

"I am Emilia, the rightful Queen of the Lands Beyond the Moon."

Chapter 25

Perhaps before going on it would be best to quickly clear up some misconceptions about the fairies that marched out then, for fairy is a word that in its common usage means nothing like the beings that met Fritz and his companions on the High Road at the gates of the fortress.

If by fairy you mean a very small magical creature with a wand and sparkling wings, rather like a flitting butterfly covered in glitter, then you are nowhere near thinking of the right sort. It is unclear where and when this whole idea of such a creature began to dominate our conceptions of fairies, but you must understand that the fairies of this tale are of a different kind altogether. You must rid yourself completely of any pictures you may have of tiny elfish sprites dancing from flower to flower in your grandmother's garden.

Now, imagine instead full-grown beings as tall as adult men, taller even, and yet more beautiful and radiant than any being that ever dwelt on Earth. These terrible beings (for they are terrible, in much the same way that the wrath of God is terrible and holy at once) walked with a majestic and stately bearing, like crowned princes or robed priests.

They were clothed in white tunics cinched about the midsection with golden belts, and these belts were not just for fashion either, but held well-used swords at their waists. Many of the fairies also wore well-shaped armor that shined like the sun, gleaming brightly on the mountain road as they reflected the Light. Their sandal-clad feet shimmered like a pale moon on the surface of a lake.

The fairies did have wings, of course, but these were no mere butterfly wings made of gossamer, but rather vast and powerful like the great wings of a golden eagle. Many of these beings had wrapped their wings about them like a cloak, and some used the thick feathers to conceal their holy faces from the travelers.

There was something at once loving and war-like about these beings in the way they stood watching the travelers. Indeed, think now of those magnificent old paintings in which Michael the great archangel tramples Satan with righteous fury, and this might give a better understanding of the fairies of this tale.

The fairies were all female as far as Fritz could tell (if such beings can be said to be male or female), and still they whispered amongst themselves in low, heavenly voices like those that Fritz had heard so long ago before the Way of Silence. He knew at once that these beings were the very same which had spoken on the wind then, and he was both glad and frightened at last to see them.

Yet confusion gripped him too at the same time, and he said to the woman in white:

"*You* are the Queen?"

"I am," said the beautiful being, "And my sister has stolen the throne from me and from Our Father."

"The old man in the dungeon!" said Hobs suddenly interrupting. He hopped and flapped his wings, "I saw him in the prison!"

"I saw him, too," said Fritz, "In a dream."

"Yes," said Emilia somberly, "The very same. Seraphina is the queen only of lies. She usurped the kingdom. Then, she hid Father to hide her sin. But there is no hiding it. And now she wages an endless war to water the flower of her rule with the blood of the Vale."

"She sent us to kill you," said Fritz and hid his face as the tears of shame rolled down his cheeks. He felt the burning poison of the wyrm Zadza in his belly with a renewed stab of pain.

"It is not your fault that you have been deceived," said Emilia, gently touching the boy's shoulder, "It is only yours now to do with the knowledge of the Truth what must be done."

She held the shining ruby aloft.

Fritz's face shone bright with the glow from the Flame of Truth.

"We must cast down the usurper. We must defeat Seraphina and reclaim the throne for you and your Father."

"It is why you were called here by the Light, the Light that came to you in the beams of the harvest moon," said Emilia.

Then, she took the faultless ruby and pressed it into the boy's belly where the wyrm had poisoned him, and at once the poison was drawn from the black wound. The venom was gone, and Fritz stood tall and the dark shame fled before the blazing stone. A veil pulled back, night turned to Day, and the boy knew Truth.

Hobs flapped his wings in a flurry of excitement and exclaimed:

"*Yoo*, y-you! You are that same royal maiden who entrusted me with the ruby! I remember now!"

The flame-haired maiden bowed her head and said, "And you have not failed in my trust, owl. This precious stone will be returned to its rightful place, when I am returned to my rightful throne."

"We must hurry back to the Castle in the Sky," said Fritz at once.

Yet Emilia placed her hand on his shoulder again and calmed him, saying, "There will be time enough for that, and much death must come before the designs of evil are undone. But before you turn back, you must go a little farther into the West, for that has always been your destination."

"But what is left that way?"

"Come and see," said Emilia.

She led the boy into the fortress with Florian and Hobs following close behind. But Reginald Dumont was left outside, still whimpering in the presence of the fairy hosts.

Queen Emilia led Fritz through the shining halls of the great fortress, and to tell of the wonders he saw there is impossible. Let us be satisfied to know that finally the boy came to the edge of the Utter West, to the highest ramparts of the fortress walls, and stared into the far distance over the face of an endless expanse of water, beyond everything, beyond all imagining.

"It is the End of Everything," said Emilia and with a soft, trembling voice of reverence, she added:

"And beyond all is the Great At Last."

There are times in the life of a young boy when he experiences things that are so utterly beyond his own comprehension that only later can he speak of them with anything like understanding.

And yet there are things still that cannot *ever* be spoken of, even after long years of reflection, for words will always be dead and simple things in comparison and to speak of such experiences at all is to approximate them. And such things

293

permit no approximation, no shadow of a comparison. Such things are sacred in the memory. They cannot be described.

They simply *are*.

Such was Fritz's glimpse of the Light upon the End of Everything and the first hint of the Great At Last.

Never had he known such happiness, such utter happiness, because for a single, sweet moment, his restless soul had known True Rest.

How long he stood there cannot be told, for that would be to speak of time amongst the Timeless.

When the group rejoined poor Reginald Dumont at the gate of the fortress, it was many hours later (the moon had disappeared and the sun took her place), and yet the man was still crying at the feet of the fairies. Queen Emilia looked sternly down on the small gentleman and said:

"Stand up, sir. You are not lost forever. Not yet. You have a chance now at Redemption, as surely as these other three have. They have marched in war against me. They meant to murder me though I am innocent, and yet now they are forgiven and go to do right. So may you! Again I say, stand, and go with them. Fight against Seraphina and you may save your sister Bijou as well."

But Reginald cried flat on his face for a long time before he ever made an attempt at standing.

Even when he struggled to his feet, the look on his face was one of fear and shame, as if he wished to bury himself in a hole and hide there forever.

"I am ready," said Fritz, his face still shining with the Light of the Great At Last. He thought of the terrors of battle ahead and yet feared them no longer for he knew that he was on the side of the Light.

"We will march at once," said Queen Emilia, "with all the fairy strength at our back."

The virtuous army went forth at the command of the maiden in white. There were no mounts, but the fairies marched on foot with the grace and power of a million cavalry men. Fritz, Florian and Hobs marched at the head of the army beside Queen Emilia, and Reginald followed behind, downcast and ashamed.

The whole host wound its way down the steps at the falls, and passed through the Ditch of Wyrms. The fiery pits and stinking sulfur seemed to pull back at their approach, to retreat in fear from the advancing army, and as Fritz marched he looked out on the blackness of the ditch and saw the deathless wyrms in the shadows with terror in their evil eyes.

Out of the Westernmost poured a righteous strength. The guards of Seraphina looked down from the outpost at the old Manor Dumont and cried in fear. Yet none fired an arrow, or tried to stop the advance, or raised the alarm at this brilliant invasion from the West. Rather the men cast away their weapons and fell on their face as surely as Reginald had done, and cried for the Doom they knew was upon them.

Yet some one of them must have gotten free and fled to Seraphina, because as Queen Emilia, the fairy army, and the companions came down out of the mountains and crossed the Vale beneath the Castle in the Sky, they were met on the plains west of Goldburg by a standing army. All the combined might of the golden city and of the Castle in the Sky stood under fluttering banners, ready for open war.

High above them in the clear blue floated the magnificent outline of the Castle in the Sky.

The armies of Seraphina were massive, and countless lance heads glimmered in the bright sunlight like noonday stars above ranks and ranks of cavalry. The snorting horses stomped their hooves anxiously on the ground, eager to charge. The lines of archers were forty men deep and stretched the length of the walls of Goldburg. The swordsmen could be numbered only by the tens of thousands, and there were enough pikemen to resist even the mightiest charge. It was a fighting force fit to trample any opponent, indeed strong enough to tear down the mountains and the moon, and the sun, and the sky itself.

Yet Fritz realized when he saw them that he was not afraid of Death, nor was he afraid of the army's power. Rather he was afraid *for* them, because he knew that all those many thousands of men were fighting on the wrong side. He was afraid *for* the Enemy. He knew that they would be thrown down, that all their collected strength would come to nothing because it went against the Light.

And he pitied them.

Queen Emilia watched the boy as the fairy army drew up its battle lines on their end of the open plain. She said:

"It is right and just to pity them, as I pity my sister. We have always wished better for her."

"We?" said Fritz.

"My Father," said the Queen. Then she smiled and said, "And Hanna and I."

"Hanna?" said Florian.

"You know the shepherdess?" said Fritz, and the memory of that kind girl shined again in his mind like sunbeams upon the meadows.

"Of course. She is our sister," said Queen Emilia, "The youngest of us three."

Fritz felt comfort in these words and said, "She was the one who sent us forward to end the evil in these lands."

The Queen nodded.

"She waited for long years in the hills, tending her sheep, watching and waiting for the boy who would come," said Emilia, "Waiting for you, Fritz."

Fritz smiled wistfully. He drew his sword and turned to face the assembled powers, all the wickedness of the ruler come down from her high place, the servant of the prince of the power of the air. The Enemy appeared unassailable, but the boy remembered the words of the Watcher so long ago. Fritz now stood ready to give his life for the defense of the right. The boy felt more frightened than he could ever remember feeling and yet he held the sword with a steady hand.

"Let us be done with it."

Chapter 26

Now comes the battle.

To tell of it in its entirety would fill books and more books and libraries of books. No doubt modern historians would enjoy that. For how many books have been written on the great battles of our own age? In a battle, a single engagement on a field, many deeds may be done, and there are deeds before, and during, and after, and deeds that beget more deeds, and deeds that might have been but never were, and deeds that were and should not have been and so forth forever.

Then come the Revisionists and everything changes.

But so as to avoid that bit of historiographical nonsense, only those events relevant to this tale will be told here. There is no need to recount the many grand individual triumphs, or the terrible individual downfalls, of the Battle of the Sisters, or the Battle of the Westward Plain, or the Battle beneath the Castle in the Sky, or the Battle of

Goldburg, or the Battle for the Lands Beyond the Moon. The point is made; even the names of this single conflict and their explanations could fill an entire book.

To those fighting it on that day, it was called simply the battle, as when black-haired Seraphina stood in her golden chariot and gave the order to Lord Otto, her trusted general:

"Begin the battle, my lord!"

Then Otto, mounted on a sleek chocolate-colored mare, called out for the archers to advance. Such was the size of Seraphina's army that the air sang with the methodical and melodious shuffle of feet and the flapping of boiled leather armor of the archers. These sounds filled the entire plain, followed by the audible click of thousands of notched arrows and the hum of drawn bowstrings, and finally the eerie twang and hateful whistle of an irrevocable act.

The arrows had flown.

Fritz watched the cloud of arrows soar high into the air and turn gently at the peak of their flight and continue their graceful arc to fall toward him and his companions. He was reminded again of the day he and Florian had watched the arrows fly in the pointless battle between Whitlee and Goldburg. How long ago that felt!

The boy knew what came next. He closed his eyes, took a deep calming breath, and waited with trembling hope as the inevitable approached. The *thumps* erupted like a chorus as the arrows sunk deep into the soil all around Fritz, and the *clings* and *clangs* answered where other arrowheads found only the fairies' metal armor and bounced away harmlessly. But over this all sang out the high notes of the arrows that bit into flesh. The cries of the wounded filled Fritz not with fear, but with a deep wish to put an end to all this bloodshed.

When the young boy opened his eyes, he looked across the plain and saw the enemy drawing another arrow. Fritz did something that was at once reckless and at the same time, the one thing that made sense to him then.

He charged.

Yelling a war cry, the young boy ran headlong toward the enemy, his sword pointed straight before him and any regard for his own life left completely behind. If it had come to it, Fritz would have fought all the hordes of evil alone, and laid down his life, and therein was his greatest victory.

Willingly, the rest of his companions followed after the boy, Florian first among them. The fox let out a series of high barks and rushed forward on the heels of his friend, teeth flashing in the sunlight, white with fury and with the frenzy of battle. Hobs spread his owlish wings and shot swiftly forward like a spear hurled by a mighty warrior.

And last of all, Queen Emilia raised her graceful hand and sent the fairy lines forward.

The thundering of their beating wings was more terrible than the pounding hooves of all the cavalry in all the battles ever fought on Earth. It was a rushing wind, or the sound of flaming tongues, and the great warriors charged forward to the greatest battle ever fought in the Lands Beyond the Moon.

Before the enormity of the fairy charge, and in the face of their splendor, Seraphina's archers threw down their bows and ran for their lives. But they could not run fast enough to escape the fleet wings of the fairies, and the wicked were cut down on the field of battle. And the lines of Seraphina's pikemen, so fit to repel a horse charge, could do nothing to turn the charge of the fairies, and many went down under the singing swords of the fairy hosts.

Now the battle was joined in earnest, and the knife work began. Fritz fought without caution, as fiercely as a young boy will when he gives his heart wholly over to some cause, and without heed for his own life, Fritz saved many other lives that day. He parried blows without knowing they were coming, and he anticipated blade swings before they were made, with a kind of free flowing swordplay that would have marveled even the masters of the art. He was everywhere and nowhere at once, and the young boy cut down many a seasoned warrior from the ranks of Seraphina's army.

Fatigue could not touch him, and though sweat and blood clouded his vision, he never tired, but fought on as the minutes turned to an hour and longer. The battle raged, with neither side gaining the upper hand, in a vicious stalemate of mounting casualties.

Then came another roar, and looking to the horizon, both sides of the battle saw that they had been joined by all the inhabitants of the Lands Beyond the Moon. Fairy messengers had flown to Whitlee and to all the villages and woods of the Vale. Likewise the messengers of the usurper-queen Seraphina had sped to rally their wicked allies.

The good arrived first.

There was the silver stallion, the leader of the Wild Horses, who the companions had once met in their War Council. Now the silver and his fellow horses stampeded into war, trampling lesser men under their strong hooves.

And all the men of Whitlee were there to fight on the side of their beloved Queen Emilia, the maiden in whom all their hopes had been placed, who had sustained them through the weary years of endless war. Now they were come to make an end of it.

But the forces of Seraphina had combined all their wicked power into one horde and had gathered its strength from every dark hole and hovel where evil hides its ugly face. There were men from every village, the kind of men who smile to your face while they slip a knife between your shoulder blades.

These were joined by every foul creature who could answer the call. The swamps had been emptied of gnomes and they swarmed over the battlefield, gnawing and hacking and slobbering in wanton rage. The King of the Bog, the Nasty Gnome himself, led them, lumbering heavily across the blood strewn field, swinging a massive mace made from the sharpened bones of unfortunate travelers who had fallen into his muddy kingdom.

Worst of all were the black shapes of the Shadows, those beasts who had descended from the Mountains of the Moon, not to help Seraphina win, but only to enjoy the evil that battles bring, to revel in the death and despair. The fairy soldiers cut these wicked beasts down first of all, for the so-called Lords of the Mountains are beasts that the righteous cannot endure. Though the Shadows were defeated and thrown down quickly, the horrific fear of them swung the battle in Seraphina's favor for a short time.

But Fritz pressed on, cutting and hewing his way through, fighting toward the pretender queen Seraphina who looked out over the plain with a contemptuous half-smile. Huddled beside her, the miserable figure of Bijou Dumont shivered in shackles.

A war horn blew and a shout followed as the cavalry of Whitlee charged with the cry:

"For the rightful Queen!"

The crash of this final charge broke the lines of Seraphina's forces, as a final wave washes out the last pillar of a pier and the whole thing comes crumbling down. Her forces began to scatter and retreat.

"You fools!" screamed Seraphina, "Fight on, you scum!"

The black-haired woman took a sword from Lord Otto's belt and lopped off the head of a fleeing soldier who passed too close to her.

"Turn around and fight, you cowards!"

But the battle was decided. The fairy hosts would not be stopped, and the soldiers and knights of Whitlee knew that victory for Queen Emilia was within their grasp.

Yet Seraphina would not surrender. Her heart hardened, and even the Flame of Truth could not burn through its wicked shell. The black-haired sorceress placed the edge of her blade against Bijou Dumont's neck and said:

"Join your power to me. Give up your will, you wretch."

"Y-y-yes, my Queen," said the depraved Dumont woman. It was Bijou's last chance to deny, to repent, and to turn away from evil, and she failed. She surrendered to Seraphina, who sucked every last bit of life from her.

You see, Seraphina needed all the black magical force she could harness because she did something then that required a desperate and maniacal (and sinful) strength. She reached high over her head and she pulled down the Castle in the Sky.

The huge mass of earth and stone, and all the buildings and its inhabitants came crashing down onto the plain. The carnage was unimaginable. Most of her own soldiers were trapped and killed under the wreckage, but Seraphina only held her chin high defiantly and cried out over the plain to her sister:

"If I cannot rule, no one can! I will tear down the very moon!"

But now that the twisted remains of the Castle in the Sky lay on the ground, the survivors came pouring out, and many who had been prisoners of the wicked queen ran out to fight on Emilia's side. The poor giant who Fritz had seen as a slave in the kitchen swung both a tree trunk and his stone mallet in vengeance, hurling aside the last remnants of Seraphina's forces. Fauns and dryads fought side by side. There was even the vixen that had made Florian's heart leap at first sight of her beauty. She was free and fighting with such ferocity that no one would come within ten feet of her if they could help it.

Fritz meanwhile fought himself to within throwing distance of the black-haired usurper, and the boy reached down, lifted a spear and hurled it at her. With a last spurt of black magic, Seraphina swatted the spear aside like a bothersome fly.

"Stupid boy!" she screamed, "Kill him, Lord Otto."

The general said, "As you wish, my Queen," and rushed at Fritz.

The swordfight between Lord Otto and Fritz happened with such speed and wildness that it would be hard to tell of it clearly. The thrusts and sidesteps and swirls and parries and blunt strikes and spins and smashes were played out to a chorus of ringing steel. You see, Lord Otto was a master of swordplay and had studied the mechanics of it for many more years than Fritz had been alive.

But the young boy was in such a state that mechanics and technique mean nothing; there is no prescribed counter to a righteous fighter with no regard for his own life. Fritz trusted in the Light to guide him and was fighting with the knowledge that Victory was already his. There was nothing that Otto could do, in the end, to withstand such an assault.

It was in this way, with reckless determination, that the boy was able to beat back the skilled general. Yet it did not allow him to defeat Lord Otto completely. Fritz swung one too many times, and Otto parried and turned aside the strike and sunk the boy's blade deep into the bloody mud. With his hand turned across his body, Fritz's side was opened up perilously to a thrust from Otto.

At that very moment, Florian leapt into the fray and threw his own body between Lord Otto and Fritz. The killing stab found the fox instead, and he fell with the sword deep in his ribs.

"Oh, Florian!" cried Fritz.

He could not see for the tears in his eyes, but he found his sword and turning, thrust it up into the heart of Lord Otto, who had been distracted by the fox.

"Florian!" cried the boy again. His heart felt as if it was the one stabbed, and his vision turned red. If he'd had no regard for his life before, now his recklessness grew to greater heights, and he rushed madly for Seraphina in her golden chariot.

The usurper-queen had lost almost all of her energy in tearing down the Castle in the Sky and was unprepared for the final charge of the boy Fritz. He leapt over the side of the golden chariot and ran her through with his sword. She screamed in pain and in the sudden realization that she had been utterly beaten, that she was lost forever.

Fritz withdrew his sword and Seraphina died, and the war was over.

The remnants of her forces scattered like chaff before the wind and many were run down and harried by the pursuing fairy forces. Those who threw down their weapons and begged for mercy were granted it. But the unrepentant were given no quarter.

Fritz ran at once back to his friend's side and cradled the broken body of the fox, his tears falling uncontrollably. He touched the sword, but the wound was too terrible, and Fritz knew. He pressed his face into Florian's blood-orange fur and wept with the sorrow of a broken heart.

"D-did we win?" said Florian weakly.

"Yes. We won."

"Good," said the fox, his voice growing fainter with every word, "I am glad of it. I am glad to have known you, Fritz. You are the best friend I ever had. And I would give my life a thousand more times to save yours."

"No, oh no, Florian! No please…" wept Fritz.

Reginald Dumont stood off a ways and even that coward cried from admiration. Hobs the owl covered his face with his wings, as did all the fairies that were close at hand. Queen Emilia was by their side now, and when the fox's eyes closed, she bowed her head in respect.

Chapter 27

There was a moment of reverent silence, and then suddenly, without warning, the fox drew the breath of New Life.

Fritz pulled away from his friend in astonishment and not a little bit of fear, and the sword fell out bloodless upon the grass. Queen Emilia only smiled down on the two.

Florian was Alive.

He lifted his head and looked about him at all the awful wreckage of the battle and seemed to be seeing it for the first time. He smiled and blinked in the sunlight and barked and nuzzled at the young boy. Fritz laughed and threw his arms around the fox and hugged him tightly.

"But how?" said Fritz, "How can this be?"

"You have won the Victory," said the Queen, "Behold the Mystery come to pass: the smallest made great! Seraphina thought she was the greatest, but in thinking so, she brought herself low. But you have given up life, and in so doing found Life more fully."

"But I do not understand," said Fritz in wonder.

"This is the greatest Love that any man or fox can have," said Queen Emilia, "To give his life for his friend."

"But what have I done to deserve it?" said Fritz, "I did nothing. I am nothing."

"Do you not see?" said the Queen, "Of course you don't deserve it! Only in knowing you don't deserve it, do you merit Love. Only in stooping can you rise. Only in venturing far into the wide unknown can you find the comfort of Home! Only in your smallness do you become great. You, Fritz, have endured and won for yourself only what you sought for others. You found Life because you faced death. You stooped and now rise. You know Home's glory because you ventured as far beyond the horizon as possible."

Fritz laughed then, and if you had asked him why in that moment, he would not have been able to tell you, but he laughed with all the easy assurance of Victory. It was pure bliss and glee and Joy. The laughter spread out through the ranks of the fairies until all the plain rocked with the sounds of happiness. Hobs joined in, and so did Queen Emilia.

And the only one who did not laugh was the poor coward Reginald Dumont.

Queen Emilia led them all to the twisted wreckage of the fallen Castle in the Sky. She held

312

up her hand for attention, and all eyes turned to her as she pointed at the mass of earth and stone. A blast sounded, that familiar trumpet that Fritz had heard in the Westernmost, and a great iron door swung open.

Out came a very old and withered Man who walked stooped with all the weight of great age. His face was like the rising sun, and His presence filled Fritz with sacred awe, for He was like the Man from his dream, the Man bound.

When the old Man reached the red-haired maiden, He took her hand and at once stood up straight as if the weight had been lifted and the years began to fall away.

"Father," said the Queen.

"My daughter," said the old Man, "How wonderful it is to see you. But where is Hanna?"

"Here," said that blonde shepherdess. Fritz was speechless, for none had seen her approach and yet suddenly there she was in all her beauty.

The old Man took both His daughters' hands. He led them forward onto the wrecked land that had fallen from the sky, and He motioned for Fritz, Florian, and Hobs to follow. The fairy army and all the rest of the onlookers, even poor Dumont, followed as well. When they had all assembled on the heap, the old Man said in a voice like thunder:

"Now let the rightful Queen of the Lands Beyond the Moon be restored!"

"But how?" said Fritz, "How when the Castle is destroyed?"

"It will be lifted up," said Emilia.

"By you?"

"Oh, no," said the Queen, "I have not the power. But lo!"

And at this there was a starburst of Light, as of that same kind that had long ago saved Fritz and Florian from the dreaded mountain monsters, a dazzling supernatural blue, brilliant as the sun, but cool as mountain springs. Fritz felt his heart cry out in sudden Joy. His soul laughed as the Light surrounded him and filled him and held him.

"Behold," whispered Emilia, yet her voice was of thunder:

"The Light is making all things new."

And at these words, the Castle in the Sky rose again into the wide blue. Higher and higher it soared, and the crumbled stones of the towers were rebuilt as if the leaves of fall had been blown back to their trees by a spring wind. The Light rebuilt the crushed golden domes and raised the walls to their former heights and restored all the glory of the floating capital.

"How can this be?" said the boy.

"All things must fall to rise."

When the Castle was restored, the assembly gathered in the courtyard before the beautiful marble man that Fritz had seen the first time he entered the Castle in the Sky. It was then that he understood that the hollow on that statue, that something missing that he could not quite put his finger on, was in the hilt of the sword and was the exact shape of a large gemstone.

Queen Emilia held aloft the shining ruby called the Flame of Truth and placed it back into the sentinel's sword, and at once the marble man lifted his burning weapon and let out a shout that shook the Lands Beyond the Moon.

Queen Emilia lifted her arm for Hobs to alight on and said, "Now, owl, you have been wise and kept your word, and done all that was asked and more."

The Queen turned to the fox and said, "And you, Florian, have redeemed the name of fox. You have been Faithful to the end."

When all this was said, Queen Emilia turned to the young boy and said, "You have done it, Fritz. You have driven out evil from the Lands Beyond the Moon."

Fritz felt his tears fall again, but they were the tears of a sorely won victory, the tears of unspeakable happiness.

"Now you must return," said Queen Emilia, "For the guardian wields the Flame of Truth, and it was for humans that the fiery sword was first placed at the gates. The faith of a child may throw wide the kingdom's gates for a time, but only for a time. But do not let your heart be troubled! One

Day this sword will be sheathed and the kingdom opened for all those who come as children, but it is not yet That Day."

"But I have failed," said Fritz, the tears falling harder now, "I still hunger. My soul still longs for…I know not what…"

"So will it always," said Hanna.

"Until you come to the Great At Last," said Emilia.

Fritz wiped his face and said, "Then will I come There One Day?"

"I am going now," said the old Man, who now did not look so old, but grown suddenly younger, He seemed to be His Own Son. As a cloud enveloped Him, He added, "I will prepare a place for you—"

With a flash like lightning, the One who was Father and Son disappeared, leaving only the shining Light, like a hovering tongue of flame that alighted upon the boy.

"You must go home now, Fritz," said Queen Emilia before the boy could say anything. She took him by the shoulder and led him to the edge of the Castle in the Sky.

Florian remained a step or two behind them. He had fallen in next to the pretty vixen that he had seen in the kitchens and again on the plains of battle. She was more beautiful in freedom than she had been as a slave, and she looked at Florian with affection in her eyes. It was clear that Florian had found Love.

Fritz stopped at the edge and said to the fox, "Will you come back with me?"

But the boy knew the answer to this question before he asked it. Florian shook his head and said:

"I have found what I sought. There is no going back."

Fritz smiled and took the fox's head in his hands and kissed his forehead.

"I will never forget you, Florian."

"Nor I you."

"Good-bye."

"Good-bye, Fritz."

The young boy turned away from his dearest friend and took Queen Emilia's hand. He whispered:

"I am ready to go home now."

In a cloud of Light, Emilia and Hanna flew him down from the Castle in the Sky, and they landed gently on the banks of the Rushing River that comes down out of the Mountains of the Moon. A small rowboat had been drawn up on the bank, and the sisters led Fritz to this and helped him into it.

"But how can I take this home over the mountains? The river flows down from the Mountains of the Moon."

His question was answered at once, as with a whispered word from the Queen the rushing waters changed direction and began to flow with all speed uphill. Fritz laughed and pushed the boat out into the swift current. Then, he turned back.

"Be kind to Reginald Dumont," said the boy, thinking of the miserable man, who in spite of everything had helped him on his adventure.

"Of course we will, my boy. There is always Hope, even for the most cowardly."

Fritz nodded. Drifting away, he waved good-bye to the two beautiful maidens.

"Good-bye, Hanna! Good-bye, Emilia!"

"Good-bye, dear Fritz! May all your days be filled with Joy!"

The Rushing River swept around a bend and over a hill and the sisters passed out of sight, and Fritz was alone.

It did not take him long to travel the many miles back home. The river rushed through the thick woods that had once swarmed with gnomes, over the flat plains of the Vale of Abundance, past the high white walls of Whitlee, up through the hills of the shepherdess and past her little cottage, and at last up and up and up into the great Mountains of the Moon. There the little boat came to a stop, and Fritz had to walk.

He made his way through the Way of Silence under the gaze of those ancient sphinxes, and down the twisting paths of the mountains. He had no fear of the Shadows as they had all been vanquished by the fairy hosts. He passed with a smile by that great stone carved all over with those strange runes that he now realized must have been made by fairies. A twinge of wistfulness and nostalgia plucked him as he passed by the old den of Florian and the place in the road where the fox had first leapt out at him.

Down he went until he came to the banks of the Milky Way. The Watcher in the Wind was not there, but Fritz passed back under the stone arch that was likewise carved with fairy writing. The great gray-orange orb of the harvest moon hung in front of the boy again.

Fritz left the banks of the Lands Beyond the Moon and swam across the white waters of the Milky Way.

When he came up on the other side, he breathed the air of Earth as one breathes the distinctive scent of one's own home after being gone on a long holiday. The smell on the air was at once familiar and yet utterly foreign. This feeling lingered with the boy for a long time after he returned home.

Fritz ran back through the woods, fearing no wolf, and went past the fairy standing stone, and over the little brook, and past the Great Oak, and then out of the wild wood to stand after all on the edge of the fallow field as he had done so long ago before his adventures.

There in the distance was the cottage of his parents and the farm where he had been born, and he looked upon them now as one would look upon an old familiar painting seen so many times before. It had rained since he had been away, and there was a small standing puddle of water between him and his parents' cottage that reflected the shape of the house. Fritz had the distinct impression then that he could not tell the difference between the two pictures, the reflection and the real thing, and he felt that stinging bitter sweetness of coming home to a place that is no longer yours.

And he wept for lonesomeness.

When the weeping ended, he went home. There was no huge welcome, no touching reunion between Fritz and Father and Mother. In fact, they did not realize he had been gone for as long as he had, and Fritz wondered that he could have so many adventures, and survive so many perils, and pass through such ordeals, and yet nothing at home had changed in the least little bit. In this was comfort and sorrow mixed.

He kissed Father and Mother, and they hugged him and loved him as dearly as always, and he they, but he was not the same boy he had been when he left on that long ago autumn night. Surely this is the tale of all journeys to adulthood, and Fritz had passed through such a journey that it could end no other way.

But lest you think Fritz grew into an unhappy man, that is furthest from the truth! Fritz grew into a joyful manhood, and did all the things that a strong and faithful man will do. He built a home not far from his parents' cottage, and he built a life there and lived it with a tender heart, and married a beautiful woman, and raised beautiful children, and had a beautiful family, and grew rich in life and Love.

The years fell away like the leaves of autumn and grew again into the bursting new life of spring, and so on and so on into gray old age.

And one quiet evening, when Fritz was a very old man, whose children's children had long ago grown into adulthood, he sat in deep thought on the porch of his old farm, looking across the fallow field toward the wild wood, and he thought he saw, dashing swiftly through the underbrush, one or two fox pups.

So he rose and took the best horse from his stable and rode off after these kits, wondering at what they could mean and feeling within him the long forgotten stirrings of a far away feeling. He rode through the wild wood, passing the Great Oak, and over the brook and past that old fairy stone now covered over with moss. And always just in front of him, he could see the fleeting forms of the young foxes.

He did not notice that he was riding beneath the pale Light of a harvest moon, or that the air floated about him with feminine voices, or that he neared those towering mountains in the West. Then, the kits vanished before him, and he came upon that starry river that flows out of the night sky, and the cup of his heart ran over with Joy and his soul cried out.

For he knew that he was bound for the Great At Last.

So Fritz crossed the waters of the Milky Way and never returned from

THE LANDS BEYOND THE MOON.

The End

Author Biography

Randal William Schmidt was born on November 17, 1988 in Corpus Christi, Texas and grew up in the small town of Sinton, Texas. He attended Texas A&M University where he earned a Bachelor of Arts Degree in English and History in 2011.

He currently teaches junior and high school English. He and his wife, Brett, are expecting their first child, a boy, in November 2014.

You can contact R.W. Schmidt at his website:

www.randalwilliamschmidt.com

If you enjoyed this book, please leave a review on Amazon or Goodreads.com.

www.ingramcontent.com/pod-product-compliance
Lightning Source LLC
Chambersburg PA
CBHW020330180626
46812CB00001B/138